CROWN &

The first book in the Ma: *Shroud* begins with the ~~thcit of the famous~~ Turin Shroud which is taken by the thieves to Paris. Medieval historian Max Quillan arrives in Paris to give lectures and learns that the sacred cloth has been stolen, days after he took part in a debate about it in Turin. He suspects the owner of the antique business adjoining his apartment block is connected to the theft. His suspicions deepen when his neighbour is found dead in her locked apartment. Tempted to play detective, aside from the police investigation, he discovers the shocking truth of who commissioned the theft, but not before Maria the concierge of his apartment is killed to silence her. Max enlists the help of her husband to expose the thieves and the mysterious buyer, but is too late to recover the Shroud.

He arrives in Edinburgh and in *Stolen Honours* becomes involved in solving another mystery linking the colourful history of Scotland's Crown Jewels with its contemporary political tensions.

To Kill a Crimewriter completes the trilogy, with a tense story which will grip readers right to the end.

About The Author

Jackson Lamont worked in journalism and broadcasting for twenty years and latterly worked as a minister in various overseas postings, among them Turin and Paris. He is the author of ten books, including biographies of John Knox and Saint Andrew; an exposé of Scientology Religion Inc. and a compilation of famous Scots *When Scotland Ruled the World*. His thriller *Hollow Rock* was set in Gibraltar where he served for seven years. He lives with his wife in Scotland and France.

CONTENTS

STOLEN
HONOURS

Chapter 1

My name is Max Quillan and I am a medieval historian, albeit one who, right now, is finding less and less satisfaction in his work.

To make life more interesting I have been travelling around as a freelance locum lecturer. I was pleased when offered a temporary post at Edinburgh University, a city I know well. I've been away for almost twenty years but the place has lost none of its appeal. I have quickly fallen back into the mindset of citizens of the capital, complaining about the throngs of tourists who seem much more numerous now despite the inflated prices.

I arrived in spring and it's now August - the month of the International Festival, which has always much to offer culturally, whether it is the official EIF or the Fringe. This year however something else has been occupying the limelight, a sensational crime which has been reported around the world. Nothing less than the theft of the Crown Jewels from Edinburgh Castle.

The Honours (as the Crown Jewels are officially known) have sometimes been in the spotlight of history and at other times neglected in the shadows. They were used for the coronation of Scottish monarchs from Mary Queen of Scots until Charles

II. From the Union of the English and Scottish crowns in 1603 until the Union of parliaments 1707, they were displayed at sittings of the Scots parliament to signify the presence of the monarch and (more importantly after the clash with Charles I) the King's acceptance of the power of Parliament.

In one of these curious rituals of British state pageantry, the monarch (or the Lord High Commissioner) signified the granting of an Act of Parliament by using the sceptre like a magic wand to touch the final print copy. Following the Union of 1707, the Honours were locked away in a room in Edinburgh Castle which was then bricked up. The Crown Jewels of England were used instead for royal rituals, giving rise to all kinds of bizarre conspiracy theories, such as the Scots' regalia had been melted down to provide dildos for Queen Anne. The truth was that they were out of sight and out of mind in their walled prison until rediscovered in 1818. They have been on public display at Edinburgh Castle ever since.

The Castle lies at the heart of the City, perched above the steep rocky cliffs of an extinct volcano. It is at once a fortress and a landmark, and the sanctuary for Scotland's Crown Jewels, the oldest crown jewels in the British Isles. It also plays host to an executive branch of the Scottish Army, a military museum and war memorial. From the east side of the Castle Rock a cobbled street called the Royal Mile runs downhill and ends at the Palace of Holyroodhouse. When I was at boarding school here, my pals and I used to visit Edinburgh Castle and enjoy the panoramic views in all directions. The Castle dominates the city like the fist of a giant hand whose wrist is the Esplanade, across which all traffic in and out of the castle must pass, over a narrow bridge and through a guarded gate. It is no wonder the fortress remained secure through the centuries (if you overlook the unwelcome visit by Oliver Cromwell).

On the Esplanade, which is similar in size to a football pitch, a vast matrix of scaffolding is erected each year to form an amphitheatre in which the Royal Military Tattoo is performed twice daily for three weeks in August. As darkness falls, out through the castle gates come a parade of military bands and performers from around the world to stage a colourful spectacle against the backdrop of the Castle walls.

The criminals who set out to steal the Honours of Scotland were later to claim they did it to restore the 'honour of Scotland'. Their bold, if not hugely daring plan was artfully conceived to coincide with a performance of the Military Tattoo. It proved to be the ideal time to pull off such a heist. Parts of the lower castle are used to assemble and marshal the hordes of bands and performers before they go out through the gate and into the middle of the amphitheatre. Performers are thus milling around inside the castle walls in various colourful uniforms.

The thieves had somehow managed to borrow, hire or steal uniforms for themselves and were indistinguishable from the Tattoo participants, some of them members of guest regiments from overseas who did not speak fluent English. Shepherding this multi-racial, multi-coloured assembly was a formidable task, made easier because the participants were used to military drills. No one had considered there might be wolves among the sheep.

Each night as the Tattoo nears the end of the performance, massed bagpipe bands and other guest personnel parade onto the arena. A lone piper is spotlighted high on the castle wall and his poignant bagpipe concludes the performance.

Fireworks then pepper the sky around the Castle rock before the spectators make their way home.

It was this moment the thieves had chosen to make their move. Earlier in the day when the Castle was open to the public they had bought tickets to the Royal Palace at the high point of the castle, where the jewels were kept in the Crown Room on the first floor. When it was closed to the public, they remained hidden within the building during the Tattoo performance wearing masks and PPE suits over their stolen uniforms. Just as the Tattoo was ending they broke the security glass and extracted the royal regalia. The theft occurred at 1035pm exactly. That was the time when the alarm registered in a control centre and the same minute at which the performance ends each evening with a firework display. The sound of the alarm was not audible in the Castle as the scene of the crime was above and away from the lower reaches of the castle where Tattoo personnel were milling around, waiting to exit after the crowds had dispersed.

The thieves had enough time to transfer their booty to a drone which arrived near them and hastily flew away from the castle with the jewels. They put the PPE suits and masks into a waste disposal bin and descended to the lower Castle area and inserted themselves among the uniformed personnel waiting to exit. The police assumed (reasonably) that the Honours and the thieves must still be somewhere inside the Castle and ordered the castle gate to be closed immediately but they were in no position to get there or to secure the wider area.

With blue lights flashing, police cars had to slow down to make their way through the thousands of people streaming down the Royal Mile at the end of the performance and there was no way that they would have been able to stem the flood and check if the thieves were among them.

The nearest place to land a drone was only a short

distance to the south, on open parkland known as the Meadows, between the Old Town and Marchmont. Conveniently the Meadows are bisected by a road where the booty was able to be loaded into a waiting van. The police found witnesses who saw men with masks covering their faces, loading something into a white van during the fireworks display. These witnesses had assumed they were part of one of the many performances in the Festival Fringe. Anyone who thinks it is odd that such activity should not be picked up as highly unusual has never been in Edinburgh during the Festival, when all kinds of loony events occur and people dress in bizarre outfits trying to solicit tourists to attend their performances in the rabbit holes of the Festival Fringe.

The van with the false number plates was picked up by cameras when it headed into the City Centre down Lothian Road. No trace was picked up of the suspect registration after that. The police assumed that it must have turned into a side street where the number plates were changed.

CHAPTER 2

Before I recount what happened to the Honours, I had better disclose how I became involved. I had studied medieval history at St Andrews University because it was one of the university's strong departments at that time. Many of my fellow students ended up being recruited by multinationals whose HR hawks circled at the end of our final year to tempt gifted undergraduates with job offers in industry.

This process went by the curious title of 'the milk round'. Most of the recruits made very successful careers for themselves and I didn't envy them that, or the fact their salaries were now vastly superior to mine. To my shame I used to laugh at the thought of my fellow medievalists grappling with the challenges of industries about which they previously knew nothing, but they have had the last laugh. I made the mistake of thinking that because I had achieved a first class honours degree in medieval history I should make a career in the same field. That choice now seemed foolish.

Some time ago I began to feel a fraud. Officially I worked as a lecturer in medieval history but no longer am inspired by history as a subject. I agree with the saying that those who do not know their history are doomed to repeat it. The proof of this is our propensity to pursue wars in the twenty first century despite the insanity that was the twentieth. History has often been PR written by the winners, agitprop in retrospect and the refuge of the chauvinist. It is important to know what ideas and people shaped our past but the twenty first century has been such a turning point in so many ways (good and bad) that I have become convinced that what I have been doing for twenty years was as irrelevant to the improvement of our civilisation as collecting matchboxes. At least until recently it has paid my bills while the matchboxes would only have helped to set light to them. The medieval world has gone for good, despite all those video games which give it new life in a digital age.

So for the past couple of years I have begun to sympathise with Henry Ford who once said 'History is bunk'.

My Damascus moment came after I spoke about the sins of the Roman Catholic church in the Middle Ages in the college at which I was then teaching. In a lecture I had remarked as an aside that little had changed over the years, as the cover-up of the recent paedophile scandals made clear. One student who was a devout Catholic had complained about me and I was carpeted by the Dean.

On another occasion, I compared the Church's extermination policy toward the Cathar religion to what the Nazis did, and found myself in danger of being 'cancelled' for hate speech or being fired. It became clear I had made the wrong career choice, so I jumped before I was defenestrated. I became a freelance lecturer, giving short courses in topics in which I had in-depth knowledge and the host university were weak. It was a way of postponing a solution to my problem. Middle age is not the best time of life for an expert on the Middle Ages to change career.

While enabling me to hide my discontent with life and medieval history by regularly moving around, these visiting lectureships in turn saved the universities from giving me a permanent post with tenure. These were as rare as hen's teeth anyway. I was easily dispensed with when cuts had to be made in the financial crisis affecting higher education, so in my new role I was useful. To begin with, my locum jobs took me to some interesting places abroad whose roots in the medieval world made them attractive places to visit. The students I taught (in English) would usually accept the novelty of my presence until they realised that the torch of learning was not burning brightly within me, but by that time I moved on to another assignment. As I said, I had become a a fraud.

Not long after launching myself as a locum lecturer, I made my next mistake. I married a French girl whom I met on holiday and ended up living in France and teaching at a university in Occitanie. The delights of living in the Hexagon wore off when my marriage was rendered threadbare after my wife took a lover. We divorced. Thankfully, no children had been conceived by this ill-conceived union. I moved back to the UK and resumed my troubadour existence.

This led me to the adventure of the Turin Shroud (see Stolen Shroud pub 2024) and no, I'm not about to tell you that this has given me a taste for becoming a private detective. Far from it. Looking back now I see that my reckless enthusiasm for solving the crime could have easily cost me my life. You will have gathered by now that like many academics, I may be well-educated and even intelligent but I lack common sense. However, common sense does not explain everything, as Hamlet said to Horatio: 'there are more things in heaven and earth than are dreamt of in your philosophy'. I think he was referring to the supernatural but I prefer the term paranormal.

Putting aside the cranks, the crooks and the credulous who are attracted to the subject, there remains a core of well-attested phenomena in psychic research which support Hamlet's remark. I am as bewildered as the next person by the advances in quantum physics which seem paranormal in themselves. Richard Feynman, one of its leading experts declared that anyone who thought they understood it – didn't. Seeking to explore this No Man's Land between science and religion, in my late teens I became a member of the Society for Psychical Research (SPR). Founded in the nineteenth century by leading scientists, it still offers a serious forum for studying the evidence for 'psi' and the more fundamental question: whether we survive bodily death in any form. My SPR membership turned out to be instrumental in finding me a place to live in Edinburgh without any supernatural intervention.

The thought of returning to Edinburgh had been an attractive one until I saw the cost of renting even a modest studio flat. When I arrived to begin my latest short-term teaching post at the University of Edinburgh, all the contacts I had from my days in the city at boarding school were long lost. Although my mother was originally from the city and my father had been at school there, both were now dead.

My father worked at GCHQ in Cheltenham where I grew up, and my mother said she always found Edinburgh stifling. I always suspected she had attended one of the schools in which Miss Jean Brodie spent her prime and she retained a capacity for enjoying mischief until a brain tumour claimed her. My father, bound by the Official Secrets Act in his work, by definition did not get up to mischief, but I loved both of them dearly and they me.

Although I started with a wish to walk to my work in a part of the University near to the centre, I soon began to research accommodation on a bus route further out. In the end it was the SPR connection that came to the rescue and helped me to acquire low-cost accommodation. In fact it was actually free. It was a tiny servant's flat on top of the magnificent building in the West End which once was the home of one of the great and good Victorians, Sir William McEwan.

He was the baron of Scotland's biggest brewery business and his name still lives on in the University's Graduation Hall. His former home at 25 Palmerston Place is now the Sir Arthur Conan Doyle Centre which acts as a hub for all kinds of activities from the New Age disciplines and therapists, yoga classes and spiritualism.

Ann Treherne, the lady who founded the Centre had given up her career in banking to pursue mediumship and was rewarded with a ghostly visit from Sir Arthur himself who prompted her to acquire the building, a story she tells in the book 'Arthur and me'. We had met at several SPR conferences and when she heard I was coming to Edinburgh for a few months she offered me a deal.

On the fourth floor of the building there was a tiny flat which, owing to a lack of accessibility and restrictions of their role as a charity, the ACD could not rent commercially. In exchange for staying rent-free in this eyrie, my tasks were to organise a programme of Tuesday Talks using my contacts in the SPR and academia, and act as unpaid janitor for the building, opening it in the morning and closing it at night. What more could I ask for? I had a comfortable bed, a tiny but well-equipped kitchen and a nice view.

The janitor task proved to be a lot of fun and the duties were light. I even learned how to bake scones which were sold in the Sherlock Holmes café. There were not as many 'cookie' people as I had feared coming about the place and I soon made more friends there than at the university, where colleagues showed little interest in a migratory bird of passage.

Now once again a bachelor, the female staff in whom I might have taken an interest were all in relationships and female students a definite no-no (at least in my morality manual). The ACD people were a diverse bunch: a retired literature professor (currently on sick leave from organising Tuesday Talks, hence the vacancy I filled); a policewoman and a psychiatric nurse, to name but three.

Ann invited me to join the board of Trustees which included an internationally known spiritualist medium, the first person I had met with such an occupation. Feeling flattered and wishing to repay something towards my free accommodation (ACD was after all a charity and run on a shoestring) I said yes and was soon meeting visiting mediums who turned out to be a very down to earth bunch. Most of them preferred to stay in hotels so I had no fear that they coveted my accommodation in the heart of the Centre which had in the past been offered as a perk to visiting speakers. The big names (since they do not feature in this story, they will remain anonymous) attracted huge audiences.

Death was clearly a popular topic. So much so that we had to move the 'demonstrations' of mediumship to larger premises which we hired on George V Bridge. I thought the term 'demonstration' rather inappropriate for talking to the dead and more suited to a food or DIY exhibition but I kept a diplomatic silence, the tenancy of my tiny flat in mind.

One night one of the famous mediums turned to me and said in his broad Glasgow accent, 'You know of course, your wee flat is haunted? In fact this whole building is. Ask Ann.' So I did.

She had not wanted to put me off staying there but in her book she details the (true) story of all the strange happenings since the ACD acquired the property. She even had ghostbuster experts come and do experiments in various parts of the building. Strange energy levels were measured but none of the ghostbusters suffered the fate of Ann's husband who was physically flung across a room in the basement.

She was a bit sheepish about failing to tell me about the ghost(s) thinking I might want to leave. Not me. I would have loved to have met them for myself but never did. It would have been just the kind of evidence that is hard to find and replicate, which (provided you accept the reality of the event) makes psi research less a science and more like a lucky dip.

CHAPTER 3

The motive for the theft of the Crown regalia did not emerge until late on the Saturday night twenty four hours after they disappeared. A video was posted on YouTube and sent to BBC Scotland and STV. No voice or face appeared in the video. It showed the jewels displayed in a location which was immediately identified by those who knew it as Arbroath Abbey, together with a written message :

'The Honours of Scotland are being held until the day Scotland is a nation again and the honour of Scotland restored. They will then be returned. This is not a ransom demand; it is we, the people, who have been held to ransom for too long'.

The message was signed 'Sine Die', who turned out to be a secretive group of Scottish separatists about which little was known up to this point except for posts on social media. They were apparently a breakaway group from the Scottish National Party which, until the last election, had bestrode the Scottish Parliament and held most of the Scottish seats in the UK parliament. A series of scandals had reduced this electoral dominance. However, support for independence in Scotland was still strong if the opinion polls were to be believed. In 2015 the separatists lost the 'indie' referendum as it was called, only by 55 percent to 45 percent.

The leaders of this new radical group argued on social media that the SNP's recent election defeat were down to the party's unwillingness to go for a strong independence message. Although they had styled themselves Sine Die, Latin for 'without a day', it was not clear whether this was exasperation at their dream of independence waiting for ever and a day, or a quote from 'Scots wha hae' one of the best known patriotic poems by Robert Burns which calls on Scots to battle for their nation, and to 'Do or Die'.

Their YouTube message echoed words 'rising to be a nation again' from the song 'Flower of Scotland' which had been adopted by the national football and rugby teams as their pre-match anthems. I always thought it ironic to see the Princess Royal happily joining in the separatist song in her capacity as President of the SRU before rugby internationals.

The choice of Arbroath Abbey as the backdrop to the video was deliberate, not simply because it was the place in which a famous Declaration was signed in 1320. It pointed up similarities between the theft and a famous incident in 1950. The Stone of Scone which sat beneath the throne on which all British kings were crowned was taken from Westminster Abbey in London by four students from Glasgow University and eventually recovered months later from the grounds of the Abbey. The Sine Die video turned out to have been shot in a studio with the backdrop of the Abbey superimposed, but the police immediately searched the Abbey and grounds to make sure. Nothing was found.

Perhaps inspired by a Compton Mackenzie story published in 1944, the theft of the Stone of Scone in 1950 aroused huge interest at the time and various conspiracy theories were circulating for years afterwards, questioning whether the stone which was returned was the original or a copy.

The four thieves were never sentenced and the leader went on to become a Queen's Counsel at the Scottish Bar. A co-conspirator who made a copy of the stone was one of the founders of the Scottish National Party. Whatever the truth, the story is worth re-telling as the stone has continued to assume an important symbolic role in national life and its theft was undoubtedly a model for Sine Die's actions.

Alleged to have been Jacob's pillow, where the Biblical figure laid his head while he dreamt of a ladder to Heaven (yes, we're in the territory of medieval myth), the quasi-sacred block of red sandstone became the symbol of Scottish pride and independence.

The nation's kings were crowned on it in Scone Abbey near Perth until 1299, when the English King Edward I (the 'Hammer of the Scots'), frustrated in his attempts to annexe Scotland, stole it. In its new home in Westminster Abbey, it was placed beneath the Coronation chair as a scornful symbol of Scotland's subservience to England. From then on it had been a thorn in the side of Scottish nationalists, symbolising England's arrogance and Scotland's shame at the loss of its sacred relic. That's the message and the myth anyway.

The saga continued into modern times. Perhaps to soften such sentiments, in 1996 the stone was returned to Scotland, and kept alongside the Honours of Scotland in Edinburgh Castle. It was taken back temporarily to Westminster to be used in the coronation of King Charles III in 2023 but since March 2024 it has been the top attraction in a new museum in Perth close to its original resting place in Scone.

The choice of Arbroath Abbey to show off their booty was also symbolic. Most Scots are sentimental and the nationalists among them are usually romantics. Who else but a romantic would think they could balance the books in an independent nation now that 'Scotland's oil' (which the SNP once used as a slogan) has gone as an acceptable source of revenue? There, I've given away my own political prejudices but don't let that spoil a good story.

So while I'm in medieval mode I might as well write about the Declaration signed in the Abbey at

Arbroath in 1320. Written in Latin by the Abbot and over fifty nobles, the Declaration came two decades after Edward had pinched the Stone. It declared that the Scots were a tribe from Scythia whom divine favour had brought to northern Britain. The document was intended to assert Scotland's status as an independent state and defend its right to use military action when unjustly attacked. It came in the wake of generations of English kings asserting hegemony over Scotland. To this end, around the beginning of the 14th century many battles had been won and lost. The eventual victor at Bannockburn in 1314 was King Robert the Bruce. During this period Bruce was excommunicated several times (once for murdering his rival in a church) by a Pope who took the English side.

The Declaration was an attempt to push home the advantage Scotland had gained but many have pointed out the 'sovereignty of the people' it claimed was an alien concept to the nobles who signed it. Others have argued it was actually copied from a similar document that the Irish used to fight against English domination. One eloquent section (probably the best known passage) was rewritten from a document by a Roman author in the first century BCE:

For, as long as but a hundred of us remain alive, never will we on any conditions be brought under

English rule. It is in truth not for glory, nor riches, nor honours that we are fighting, but for freedom – for that alone, which no honest man gives up but with life itself.

Curiously this document disappeared from public discourse for centuries until it resurfaced around the end of the 17th century during the Glorious Revolution. Today its ideas were finding new expression in groups like Sine Die and those who support them.

CHAPTER 4

Living above the ACD gave me two huge bonuses. The free flat I have already mentioned. The second bonus arose out of the Tuesday Talks. I noticed that a regular attender was a very attractive lady of a certain age who had no wedding ring and a figure that was enhanced by the close-fitting dresses she wore under her Burberry raincoat. At first I thought she was Carol Vorderman who, since she left 'Countdown' had seemed to be everywhere on television, even in the adverts.

A few years back Carol said she had given up on monogamy and instead preferred what she called 'special friends'. Like her, this lady had long dark hair and brown eyes and obviously shared my interest in psychic research. Maybe, I mused, I could volunteer to be a special friend. So I introduced myself and discovered she was not Carol V. Her name was Rosamunde Michelle and she was a KC and criminal advocate (the job title by which barristers are known in Scotland). We were soon enjoying more than Tuesday Talks together and eventually became lovers.

There was another bonus in the fact that she lived just round the corner in Eglinton Crescent, diagonally across the road from the ACD Centre.

Our activities both social and romantic were based more in her one bedroom flat than in my attic flat above the ACD not because Rosamunde would have been spooked by the resident ghost since she was obviously interested in psychic phenomena.

She simply didn't like climbing four flights of stairs in her stiletto heels which would have proved dangerous for the descent down the magnificent spiral staircase in the centre of the building. For all their Enlightenment genius, the Georgian and Victorian builders of posh apartments in the New Town and West End did not manage to put in elevators (or shafts that might be used to insert them in later years). The guard-dogs of modern Conservation see to it that none will ever be built.

Rosie, as I soon learned to call her, was amusing company, highly intelligent, and her evident charms made her very successful with juries when she exercised her profession in defending the criminal classes of all shades of collar: blue, white and dog.

She had never been married but in her wilder youth had given birth to a child who had been adopted. She told me about that once when she had too much to drink. Talking about it brought such a frown to her face and a sharp tone into her voice, that I knew it still caused her pain and I never raised it again. In earlier years she could have had her pick of the male advocates but said she found socialising in 'the charmed circle' to be suffocating as so many of them were either boring or narcissistic. ('Up themselves' was the exact expression she used).

The bitchy ones referred to her as La Belle Michelle or the Belle of the Bar but she won out by simply taking that as a compliment. She preferred doctors to lawyers, she said, but the two relationships she had had with members of the medical profession had foundered when they gave more time to their patients than to her. Noted. As a part-time lecturer and janitor, I reckoned I could find enough time for her sparkling company. Our relationship had already lasted two months when the robbery at the Castle took place.

As it happened, her best friend from schooldays was in charge of the police investigation and as you will learn later in this story, Rosie was to be given the task of defending the people accused of the crime. Yes, Edinburgh is a small world especially in the field of the law, but it is not usually a corrupt one. Despite appearing on opposite sides in many court cases Rosie and DCI Helen Dyer (her childhood friend) could score points from one another and enjoy a drink together afterwards. Since most of Rosie's clients were guilty anyway (whether or not they pleaded that way), when she managed to get an acquittal or a 'not proven' verdict (that peculiarly Scottish option of a no score draw) there were usually no hard feelings on Helen's part. Most of her police colleagues viewed the 'not-proven' verdict with the same disgust as football fans do when the opposition score a winner in extra time.

When I met her, over drinks in Rosie's flat on Sunday night, two days after the Castle theft, DCI Helen Dyer had been having (in her words) 'a helluva day' and asked Rosie to mix her a Negroni. The Sine Die video had appeared online overnight on Saturday and the crime at the Castle had become a political sensation and in turn had raised a media storm. I could easily see how that was making Helen's job more difficult. To my surprise she disclosed to Rosie and me that the declaration of the 'Tartan Terrorists' (as the media were inevitably calling them) actually came as a relief. I rather liked her forthright attitude instead of the mealy-mouthed 'police speak' used by some police personnel when they address a camera, using expressions like 'operational resources' or when they feel they need to say 'our thoughts are with the family' in order to seem sympathetic. I prefer to take the latter for granted.

Helen trusted Rosie enough to trust me and expressed freely her opinions about the Sine Die video and the motive for the theft.

'The video is genuine but the background has been CGI'd on.'

'What's CGI?' Rosie interrupted.

'Computer stuff. Background that is edited digitally behind a newsreader to make it look as if they are at some high viewpoint when they're actually in a TV studio. So that bit is faked but the crown and jewels are the real deal. Naturally we checked out the Abbey but frankly, I'm relieved it's a home grown effort.'

'Relieved?' repeated Rosie questioningly.

Her friend was used to the to and fro of their dialogues and continued her explanation.

'Yes, imagine if the jewels were being trafficked overseas to be sold or if there had been a ransom demand. In the first case we don't have the resources to go checking around the usual fences for stolen gems internationally or the private auctions run by villains. I just don't have that expertise either. As for a ransom – if they had wanted money who would have paid it? The King? The Scottish government, bless them? Or will they blame it all on Westminster as usual. Ha Ha. The Nationalists can't get away with that this time when it was their own buggers who did it.'

Helen was clearly not an SNP supporter. She went on 'When it comes to money, half of the public would say good riddance, we're not paying millions when we can't even fund the decrepit health service. The whole thing would then become a political punch-up. At least we know these buggers will want to keep the stuff in Scotland and so we'll start by looking here.'

There followed a speculative conversation among the three of us about where Sine Die might be keeping the Honours. I favoured the idea that they saw themselves as Robin Hood figures, romantics with a feel for symbolic gestures. They would choose somewhere significant like Culloden battlefield or Bannockburn. Rosie reckoned Scone or St Andrews or the island on Loch Leven where Mary Queen of Scots was once held prisoner.

Helen was sceptical. 'Activity around all these places would be spotted. They would need to bury the stuff and we've already checked most, if not all these places for suspicious activity.'

'What if they've taken them abroad?' I raised my eyebrows mockingly. 'Even England?'

'Nah. The odds are they will be in some lock-up in a quiet mews lane in Edinburgh. Reduces the chance of getting caught shifting them. They could have done the transfer within minutes of getting away from the Meadows. And swapped their fake plates at the same time. Some poor bugger in my unit is going to have to trawl through the camera footage of all the white vans in Edinburgh that night. Good old fashioned police work.'

'Don't the Honours belong to the Crown Commissioners?' I said.

'Well they call themselves the 'Commissioners for the keeping of the Regalia' or some such nonsense. It's only three people who have big titles and other jobs. Historic Environment Scotland are meant to manage the things but obviously they haven't done that very successfully. Any time I've had to deal with that set of priss pots and it has been a nightmare. I'm not going to get involved in all the bureaucratic wrangles of who owns what. My priority is to find who these three buggers are, and where they got their drone. Plus identify their accomplices with the van and where they have hidden the stuff. Then the King will make me a Dame.' She grinned.

'You're a dame already,' jousted Rosie. 'And this is a real pantomime anyway.'

Helen growled and grinned simultaneously, Eartha Kit style. 'I'm also going on a mole hunt. Someone inside that Castle had to have given them the low-down. Perhaps not an inside job but maybe an independence sympathiser. We're looking at Nationalist groups obviously. But somebody with military connections must have given them that drone. It wasn't one of those wee toy things you get on the internet to play with in the park. The payload must have been heavy. One of my sergeants is researching drones and who has them at their disposal.'

I liked her forthright style but she was careful not

to disclose any more about the police operation. When I remarked it was not the first time the Honours had gone missing she asked me to elaborate. 'You're a historian, Max. As Rosie knows, I was no good at history at school. We asked for stuff on the jewels and back came a pile of unreadable papers that I haven't had time to look at. Spare me that. Fill me in.'

It so happened that the Scottish Crown Jewels date back to the medieval period which is my speciality and I had also looked up Wikipedia that morning, so I tried my best to make it interesting. Helen, I suspect, was easily bored. 'Are you sure you want this?'

'It will beat reading all that paperwork. Go on, try me.'

'Well, as you know the basic Honours consist of the Crown of Scotland, the Sceptre, and the Sword of State. The present gold crown was made in Scotland in 1540 but the earliest depiction of a Scottish king wearing his kit was King Edgar around 1100, wearing crown, sceptre, sword and ring. This all disappeared South after the English invasion of 1296. New regalia were made in subsequent centuries and the present set were first used together at Mary Queen of Scots coronation. Then from 1603 when Scottish and English monarchs were the same guy, until the Union of parliaments in 1707, they were taken to sittings of the Parliament of Scotland to signify the monarch's presence and their acceptance of the power of the Parliament. Remember all the trouble when Charles I wouldn't play ball with parliament?'

'And got his head chopped off,' put in Helen.' And we got Cromwell as Lord Protector,' she added, now showing off.

'Well, later in the same period when Cromwell's army were advancing fast into Scotland in June 1651 the Honours had to be moved out of Edinburgh Castle. They were taken north east to Dunnottar Castle on the coast south of Aberdeen. It was a real cloak and dagger operation. They were brought to Dunnottar, hidden in sacks of wool, and Ogilvie, the lieutenant-governor of the castle, was given responsibility for their defence. In November 1651, Cromwell's troops called on him to surrender, but he refused so they blockaded the place. His smart lady wife and the wife of the local minister at Kinneff smuggled them out and away. One story has it that over the course of three visits to the castle she hid the crown, sceptre, sword and scabbard amongst sacks of goods. Another story says that the honours were lowered from the castle onto the beach, where they were collected by her servant and carried off in a creel of seaweed and subsequently buried under the floor of the Old Kirk at Kinneff. They remained there for ten years until the Restoration of Charles II in 1660, when they were returned to Edinburgh Castle after Charles was crowned.'

'Well done these girls,' exclaimed Helen. 'I like happy endings.'

'Well actually it wasn't the last time they disappeared. During the debates in the Scottish Parliament in 1707 on the Treaty of Union, rumours spread that the Honours were to be taken to England and melted down.' (I missed out the bit about the dildos which I knew they would have enjoyed too much and it was fake news anyway). 'When the Scottish Parliament closed in March 1707, the Honours no longer had any practical use, so they were taken to the Crown Room in Edinburgh Castle, where they were safely locked away in a big oak chest, the doorway of the Crown Room was walled up and there they stayed for a hundred years.'

'You're joking!'

'No, I'm not. Have you read any Walter Scott?'

'I have,' said Rosamunde. 'But I don't recall that story.'

'Scott was a hugely influential guy at the time. He was involved when they unblocked the wall in 1818. He master-minded the visit of King George IV in 1822 and stage-managed the whole thing. He even persuaded the king to adopt Highland dress and symbolically touch the regalia. The whole visit was worthy of an opera and is sometimes said to be the birth of 'tartan kitsch'.'

'This is very entertaining,' said the policewoman. 'Is that the end of the story?'

'Not quite. During the Second World War - you'll like this bit, Helen - the Honours were hidden at the Castle owing to fears they might be lost if the UK fell to Germany. The Crown and Stewart Jewels were buried under the floor of a lavatory, while the sceptre, sword and wand were hidden inside a wall. The only officials who knew of the hiding places were the King and three others who included the Governor General of Canada. In June 1953 the regalia were presented to the newly crowned Elizabeth II at a National Service of Thanksgiving in St Giles' Cathedral. The wily old fox, Sir Winston Churchill, who was then Prime Minister, advised the Queen to dress informally to avoid it being seen as a 'Scottish coronation'. The Crown was placed on her coffin when she lay in state in St Giles in 2022 and the Honours were presented to Charles in 2022 when he came North on his succession. I think that brings you up to date.'

'Thank you, Max.' said Helen. 'If you'd been our history teacher. I would have paid more attention.'

CHAPTER 5

On Monday, three days after the theft, I paid my own visit to the Castle. It was to fulfil a long-standing lunch date with an old school chum, Jordy Ochterlonie who became an army major. Now retired, he was working part-time in one of the regimental museums housed in the upper castle buildings. We had originally agreed to meet in the Royal Scots Club in the New Town but I was curious to visit the scene of the crime and persuaded him to change the venue. It was simpler for him anyway to come to the castle gate and vouch for me than for him to go downtown. The police were taking a long time to check the crime scene and the Castle was still temporarily closed to the public. I was looking forward to getting the inside story from his perspective.

I got to know the Castle well when I was at a boarding school in Edinburgh. All the pupils were taken on an annual outing to the Tattoo (this was said to be voluntary but none of us dared opt out). The purpose I always suspected was to interest us in a career in the armed forces. It did not work for me, but I enjoyed the show nevertheless. On other days, to escape school for a few hours I used to go up to the castle to enjoy the views of the city, eat a snack and experience the one o'clock gun up close as it fired over the city. In my schooldays it was louder than it is now, Health and Safety having put mufflers on the blank shells which are used. Entry to the castle then was free but now a hefty fee is charged to those who want to visit and pay extra to view the Honours of Scotland.

Today for the first time in its colourful history it was a crime scene. Helen Dyer had told me to take my passport as photo ID. It was good advice as several questions about the purpose of my visit were asked in order for me to pass through the entrance gate. Jordy had alerted them of my visit and was waiting just inside the gate. As we walked up the cobbled road he mentioned that he had thought he might have had to cancel my visit.

'I even wondered whether I would be allowed in to work but in fact they wanted me here. Everyone – and I mean everyone, even the Governor - are being asked to account for their movements on Friday evening and whether we know anything about this Sine Die group.' He pronounced it the way our Classics master would have done, whereas many of the media reporters were pronouncing it as 'Syne Dye'.

I told him I had met DCI Dyer the previous evening at Rosamunde's flat. He said he had already been questioned by her.

'Quite a straight talker, isn't she? Reminds me of that redhead who was Inspector Lynley's sidekick in the TV series. She gave me the third degree yesterday. Especially when she heard I had been in the Gulf war. Whether I knew anything about drones or who might have access to them. It was quite strange to be on the other side of the desk. In the Gulf I had to interrogate suspected Republican guards among the Iraqi POWs.'

I found it difficult to imagine Jordy as an interrogator but perhaps his impeccably polite manner would have worked where shouting and waterboarding did not.

'I daresay the police wouldn't find many Nationalist sympathisers among your lot, Jordy. Certainly not you.' (I knew him to be a Tory of the deepest blue).

'Well actually you might be surprised. A fellow in one of the regiments was so incensed by the Defence cuts a few years ago, he joined the Nats to campaign to save the Scottish regiments.'

Since Jordy's job was to run the archives in one of the regimental museums, it must have been demoralising for someone as proud of the history of Scottish regiments as he was, to see them amalgamated, decimated and reduced to a single fighting force when previously there had been at least twenty regiments after World War II, drawing their recruits and conscripts from all regions of Scotland.

'What's the gossip here in the Castle about the heist?' I asked him. 'Any chance of knowing how they managed it and got away?'

Jordy repeated what I had heard from DCI Dyer, that the thieves had used the firework display to cover their entry into the Crown Room and had employed a drone to take the jewels out. Then they made their escape with the Tattoo participants dressed in uniforms of one of the foreign regiments. 'The police took the names of everyone who went out of the gate after the theft and photographed them all. At that point they didn't know about the drone and assumed the thieves would be trying to take them out. Took ages but it was necessary as none of these performers were carrying proper ID. I think the culprits may have stolen the passes as well to get in and out. There was an awful fuss when they arrested a chap from one of the guest foreign regiments because he didn't have his pass. Chap didn't speak much English but he was legit. There were actually several foreign groups taking part. Don't ask me what they were doing. I have seen so many Tattoos over the years with my family that I stopped going a few years back after the boys had grown up. Seen one, seen them all.'

I sensed Jordy was reaching the point of seeing retirement as a positive option. The low morale in

the army had affected even military men like him
whom I remembered being always enthusiastic about
joining the army when he was in the cadet force
at school. I usually kept my quasi-pacifist views to
myself when we met over the years but I could easily
sympathise with having given loyalty and energy to
an institution which was now in decline. As I was
having a mid-life crisis of my own, I was not about
to share how I had fallen out of love with history.
On second thoughts, his raison d'etre here was the
history of the Scots regiments so I decided that
belittling history was undiplomatic and I would tell
him instead about my new job as a janitor and the
new lady in my life.

We had just reached the halfway point in our
climb and were walking past the crew preparing to
fire the one o'clock gun, pointing north from the
battlements toward Princes Street and in the distance
to the Firth of Forth and Fife.

'Still firing the gun, I see, despite everything,' I
remarked.

'Oh yes. Outwardly we want to give the
impression of business as usual. Castle re-opens to
the public tomorrow. Tattoo back on tonight. Two
shows. There was a lot of ticket money lost this
weekend. Helluva fuss if they close down the Tattoo
and the Castle. Can't let these chappies be seen to
win. Of course you know that the Crown Room isn't

anything to do with the army. It's run by Historic Scotland.'

I nodded in agreement, anxious to sympathise. We had reached the highest point of the castle ground on our walk and I could see the crime scene tape around the Royal Palace building ahead blocking our progress. We had to make a turn to avoid it.

'You said you wanted to have a look at the War memorial and find your grandfather,' Jordy reminded me. 'We could do that now before a modest lunch in our even more modest canteen. At least you get a good view.'

'Ideal,' I replied. My great-grandfather died at the Somme in 1916 and his name was among the thousands around the walls of the museum which Robert Lorimer had designed. It opened in 1927 and since then had never been short of visitors. Many of them are from overseas who come to find an ancestor's name and although surprised by its simplicity are invariably awed by its atmosphere. I had not visited it since my father took me there while I was still at school. Now middle-aged I found myself strangely moved when I looked around the bronze walls at the names of the young men whose deaths had marked a turning point in the brutal history of humanity.

Over lunch (which was as disappointingly modest as Jordy had warned me) I was anxious to get more insider gossip about the theft. 'What do you think is going to happen now, Jordy? That Sine Die video is genuine even if the backdrop is not and was perhaps put there to mislead. So far the police have not seen anything that might identify the trio.'

'Oh, but they have,' Jordy replied brightly. 'That's the thing. The police took photos of all those leaving the Castle and three names were not among the approved personnel. They have their faces. It's a matter of time before the police arrest them.'

He had a point. He showed me that day's Daily Record newspaper which had a big spread on the group calling themselves Sine Die. The article had been written after the video emerged and was inevitably short on detail and names and had plenty of conspiracy theories with no evidence to back them up. According to 'inside sources' the group had become fed up with the SNP leadership and decided that radical action was required to grab public attention and gain sympathy for the cause of independence. They apparently hold meetings in secret and are careful not to copy groups like the eco-terrorists Extinction Rebellion who, by blocking traffic or glueing themselves to offices of oil companies, have mostly lost public sympathy rather than gained it. Heavy jail sentences were handed out to some of them last year for blocking the M25 round London. The article went on to quote some of the colourful Sine Die rhetoric in previous postings on social media, which they access under false names via TOR and VPN accounts that cannot be traced. The newspaper had nothing to offer on the identity of the three men who had bluffed their way into the Castle.

I thanked Jordy for lunch and made my way back down to the University where I had a lecture to give on the 'mysterious disappearance of the Picts', but was much more fascinated by the mysterious disappearance of the Crown Jewels.

Chapter 6

That night I stayed in my flat watching television and went to bed early. The arrest of three men came during the night and was quickly made known via radio and television stations. As I ate my muesli and fruit, DCI Helen Dyer's brief statement was read out by the presenters.

'Following a police operation three men have been taken into custody in connection with the theft of the Honours of Scotland from Edinburgh Castle on Friday night. Their ages are 33, 25 and 42 and they are being questioned at an Edinburgh police station. No further statement will be issued until a media briefing at Police Headquarters at Fettes Avenue tomorrow at 10am.'

I wondered whether the straight-talking Helen would adopt the same manner she had shown during our conversation on Sunday night when she met the media tomorrow. Or would she be forced to use the dead-pan, straight-bat manner and the vocabulary of police-speak? I was fascinated to know how the men would plead. Would they own up and return the jewels and hope for clemency? After all, no one had been injured and presumably the jewels were undamaged. They were no doubt preparing to use any trial as a publicity ploy for their campaign.

Or would they stay silent and refuse to talk? The police could play hard and try to bring terrorism charges which would lengthen the period during which they could question the men but that still seemed to me unlikely. The Stone of Scone thieves had not been even tried for their offence. However in 1950 the political climate was entirely different. In today's more volatile political atmosphere, trying to accuse Scottish separatists of terrorism would be likely to bring a backlash, perhaps even make martyrs out of them.

Up to this point I had not considered the obvious alternative that the trio might plead 'not guilty', or that the men arrested might actually be innocent. Like many people I too readily assumed that the police do not usually make mistakes when they arrest and charge someone, and the Prosecutors do not put innocent people on trial. In the light of the Post Office scandal and several other appalling miscarriages of justice in recent years, I realised my automatic acceptance of the guilt of those arrested was perhaps a naivety.

The arrest of the three men was perhaps only the beginning of a wider operation. What of the confederates who drove the white van and had collected the drone? Would the trio shop their mates? Unlikely. Someone had supplied the drone, possibly a person with military connections. Was there a mole inside the castle who had helped them with inside knowledge? This was shaping up to be a story worthy of the Wizard of the North himself, Walter Scott, who had played a part in the recovery of the Honours two hundred years ago.

It certainly beat the one I was working on, the story of the Picts. They were long-lost people of North and East Scotland, whom I was currently researching and giving seminars about in my temporary post. I was conscious that much of what I was telling my students must seem nebulous to them. The problem was that the Picts had disappeared permanently as a distinct people around a thousand years ago, like the Cathars in southern France in the same period, but for very different reasons. I had given lecture courses about the Cathars (most recently in Paris) and in comparison the Picts were a lot more elusive. Little was known about them with certainty and most of that was written in stone. Literally. Hundreds of stones dotted around the countryside inscribed in a language that had disappeared with the Picts. I was planning a trip to the Pictavia museum in Brechin to see some of the stones when my phone pinged with a text from Rosie.

'Can't make our RV tonight. Something big has come up. Let yourself in and eat what's in the fridge.

I'll be home when I can. I have something to tell you. Kiss you. Rxx.'

I polished off a pork chop fried with apple slices, some leftover ratatouille and a microwaved potato. I had not presumed to open any of her rather fine collection of clarets and relied on a wine box of Merlot in the larder to wash it down. As I was doing the dishes, I saw her desk diary open on the kitchen worktop and it gave me an idea. We had been an 'item' for two months now and my feelings for her were strong. The idea came to me of doing something romantic, any excuse would do.

Perhaps her birthday was coming up but I did not know the date. The anniversary of our meeting was too far in the future, that is if our relationship would last that long. So I sifted through the pages of the desk diary to see if there was a clue about her birthday.

I saw that on one day every month, the word 'Longforgan' was written. I recalled that this was where someone lived who had been at school with me. Although I had never been to his home, I once saw as we all packed up at the end of term that he had an address in 'Castle Huntly Road' written on the label of his trunk. I wondered then if he might actually live in a castle. I remembered him not because he went on to become a famous television presenter on politics and wrote a brilliant book on modern British history, but rather because he had taken out a girl on whom I had set my sights and I lost out. I am not a jealous person by nature but the memory of that time aroused unaccustomed emotions which I found myself transferring to my relationship with Rosie. Did she perhaps have someone else in Longforgan? I had never asked her about her prior attachments and probably did not want to know, since we were both mature adults. However, my emotional reaction was telling me that I cared a lot about her and did not want our relationship to end. I made up my mind to find out when her birthday was and what her connection was with Longforgan.

That evening proved not to be the best time. When she breezed through the door at 11pm, I offered her a glass of wine but she declined. 'No, I need something stronger. So will you, when I tell you my news.'

I poured her two fingers of malt from a decanter on her marble-topped drinks table and looked up expectantly. She smiled. No, she actually grinned. 'I've been asked to represent the so-called Tartan Terrorists when they come to trial. All three of them. And I've accepted.'

'But you're not even a nationalist!' I blurted out, then realised this remark might seem to suggest that she was not up to the job. 'This case has political overtones and you don't share their politics.'

'Yes it could seem political but that's the point. It's a criminal case not a political one. Technically it will be treated as theft, just like housebreaking. In the Faculty of Advocates we operate a taxi-cab system so that if you're free you get the next case in line when someone is charged. That's not happening this time. They want someone outside the SNP web. You weren't here at the time but the former leader of the SNP, First Minister Alex Salmond was put on trial for sexual hanky panky a few years back. Now that was political. It was orchestrated by his female successor, a nasty wee woman and her acolytes. And do you know what he did? He hired the Dean of the Faculty of Advocates who had been a parliamentary candidate for the Labour party, to represent him and was cleared of all the charges. The two of them weren't even friends and actually disliked one another. Everyone knew it.

The trio I am about to have as clients obviously think the same thing could work for them. After all, I'm known at the Bar for having tried to get a group together called 'Advocates for the Union' at the time of the Indie referendum in 2015. It bombed partly because most of the people in line for promotion knew that crossing the SNP was not a good career move. The Crown Office controls judicial appointments and that woman managed to get a lot of her people in high places. She's gone now, thank God, but the SNP are still very powerful.'

I was about to interrupt when her enthusiasm boiled up again. 'Besides, having spoken to their solicitor, I can tell you that the case against my clients at the present time is pathetic. Unless the Crown can get their fingerprints on the jewels, and they do not have a single jewel, we should win. Of course I'm not counting any chickens but I'm looking forward to the case. If it goes well it could become my passport to a sheriffdom and out of the treadmill at Parliament House. Like you I need a change of direction. I just hope anything I'm offered will be in travelling distance of this place.' Her face clouded briefly. 'The only thing that worries me is Helen's reaction when she hears that I've taken the brief. This will put me in a position when inevitably I will have to challenge the police work. I hope she understands. She did in the past, but it's the first time she has had charge of a big case and I've been leading for the opposite side.'

I tried a reassuring tone. 'You two have been friends a long time, Rosie. It'll be fine. I suppose from what you're saying your clients will plead not guilty. I know this all confidential and I promise I won't breathe a word but are you able to tell me anything more? For example, how do they explain coming out of the castle immediately after the Honours were taken?'

'Yes, Max, you're right. I can't say any more about any of this at this point. What I can say is that the Crown will have to show how three men carrying nothing but a banner saying 'Only a fool likes London rule' which they wanted to display during the Tattoo, have committed a crime. Maybe a cheeky bit of trespass. But where were the jewels?'

'They gave false names. Isn't that evidence of intent?'

'Intent to get out of there when the balloon went up. They might have been accused of something they didn't do.'

I could see Rosie was already rehearsing her case for a not guilty verdict and I did not want to dampen her spirits. She looked exhausted and so we went to bed, spooned together in embrace with her facing away from me. I could feel she was still wide awake. At 5am her phone rang, she left the room to answer it and I fell back to sleep. When I woke up in the morning she was gone.

CHAPTER 7

Shuttling between Rosie's flat and my own meant I needed a razor and toothbrush in the place in which I woke up. In five minutes I had used both and gone round to Palmerston Place to open up the ACD building. My morning ritual of eating fruit and muesli mix for breakfast is usually accompanied by radio news, not the lightweight fare offered by sofa-sitters of television morning programmes. That morning BBC Radio Scotland was headlining a development in the case of the Crown Jewels. Two more arrests had been made overnight and a white van taken into custody.

That gave me a clue as to why Rosie had received a phone call at 5am. I gathered she was about to embark on a long day so I texted her 'good luck'. Fortunately before I set off for the Pictavia Centre in Brechin, I checked it out online and discovered it had closed permanently. My intention had been to gather more information and photographs of Pictish stones and so I looked for alternative places where I might find others. The Picts in their heyday were concentrated in the north east of Scotland and Fife. Many of the villages in Fife I remembered from my student days carried the tell-tale prefix 'Pit'

(Pittenweem, Pitscottie) which testified they were once part of the Pictish kingdom. In St Andrews itself the cathedral museum houses the Pictish Sarcophagus, a splendid box-like stone artefact adorned with Pictish symbols. It took me an hour and a half to get there and after photographing the sarcophagus, another hour's drive to get across the Tay Road Bridge and along the coast into Arbroath.

My visit there was partly out of curiosity to see the famous Abbey but also to buy some Smokies fresh from the smokery of the veteran Mr Spink next to the harbour. I have never been there but I knew Rosie had raved about this smoked haddock delicacy. Arbroath Smokies can be used to make a quiche or a soup or I could simply add them to a salad for our next meal together. Mr Spink showed me the room in which he smoked the fish next to his shop. I left now much more knowledgeable about Smokies which require a capital 'S' as they have been granted an 'appellation'. It was bizarre to learn that the once busy fishing harbour of Arbroath was now a ghost port and Mr S's fish were landed at Peterhead and came south by train. So much for fresh fish.

I had time to enjoy a late lunch at the Old Boatyard, an excellent restaurant overlooking the harbour, and then drove north to Aberlemno to photograph more Pictish stones there. I already had photographs of several 'brochs', in which the Picts lived and of the Crannog reconstructed in Loch Tay to illustrate this form of off-shore dwelling which protected the Picts from predators. Some historians claim their form of kingship was more institutional than personal and it came through the female line, but I tended to think this was an attempt to project more modern ideas onto them. Much as I would have liked to gather more facts about the Picts for my students, there is not a lot to know and some of it is under question. Bede's 'historical myths' have been picked apart by better historians than I am. Besides, this story is not about them.

By taking a faster route back to Edinburgh after joining the A90, I drove past Forfar down to Dundee and along the dual carriageway towards Perth. Soon after Dundee I saw the signs for the village of Longforgan which the road by-passes. Beyond the village, presumably down 'Castle Huntly Road', I saw the tower of a mock castle protruding from the flat landscape which extends all the way to the north bank of the Tay.

When I got to my flat in the ACD building it was too late for DCI Helen Dyer's 5pm media conference which had been carried live by BBC Radio Scotland. But I caught plenty of clips of it on the other news channels. Apparently the police had been active not only arresting people and questioning them but had actually been in Angus at the same time as me, at a building in the Angus Glens. These valleys descend southwards from the Cairngorm mountain range, on whose northern flank lies Royal Deeside and Balmoral Castle, the summer retreat of the British Royal family.

The building which the police raided was a redundant church in Glen Clova. The Kirk, as the Church of Scotland is often called, had exercised a dominant role in Scottish culture until now. Sharp decline in membership and finances had led to it closing churches and selling off many of the buildings. Amalgamations of congregations and groupings of the small rural ones had proved no longer radical enough to stem the ebbing tide.

The Glen Clova church building had been sold to a Trust which turned out to be Sine Die under another name. They apparently had used it to store publicity materials and hold meetings of their members away from prying eyes. It had not been enough for them to escape the attention of Special Branch, which takes an interest in groups such as theirs. Perhaps by infiltration or previous surveillance of the group the police had found the place and searched it. They got a surprise.

The members of Sine Die had a sense of humour. They obviously had heard the story of how the Honours had been hidden beneath the floor of Kineff church nearly four hundred years previously.

When the police removed a stone covering a crypt-like space, they found a crown and a handful of jewels. Unfortunately for the police, the Crown was made of papier-mâché and wire. The Jewels were cheap costume jewellery. Red faces all round. Special Branch and DCI Dyer's team would no doubt have wanted to keep this information quiet but when other members of Sin Die learned about the raid, they leaked the story. It dominated the next day's newspapers and made the police look foolish.

As a King's Counsel, Rosamunde was not involved in representing the suspects during their police interviews. Her role as an advocate would be to conduct pleadings in the High Court when the case eventually came to trial. First the men would appear in a Sheriff Court and KCs rarely appear at this stage.

The men were represented at the police interviews by a well-known Glasgow solicitor by the name of Musa Iqbal who had an unerring talent to land high profile cases involving victims of police violence or challenges to extradition. All of these usually attracted much media coverage. Musa would be seen standing beside his clients for the cameras and occasionally step forward to speak on behalf of those who were uncomfortable with the spotlight (as he was decidedly not). He was a cousin of one of the ministers in the SNP government but that had not stopped him challenging its conduct on a couple of occasions.

Once the three suspects were charged, Mr Iqbal would represent the men at the Sheriff Court where the presumption was that they would be released on bail pending trial. There were good pragmatic reasons why the Fiscal was not likely to oppose bail. Firstly, Scottish prisons were vastly overcrowded and granting bail had become the default policy unless by releasing suspects public safety was threatened. Secondly, Sine Die were likely to be portrayed as martyrs if they remained behind bars. After being released on bail, they would be forbidden to speak about the case until they came to trial. Additionally it would mean that the hunt for the jewels would be intensified and if they were found, the case against the thieves would be much stronger. Prosecuting murder without a body is always difficult. In this case it was theft without the booty.

CHAPTER 8

The morning after she had faced the cameras, DCI Helen Dyer was fizzing. The leak about the fake crown and jewels in Glen Clova had meant most of the newspapers and social media were having a field day. Those twitterati who supported independence wrote comments in support of Sine Die's action and there were a lot of them. 'PC Plod digs for treasure-and finds junk jewels' was typical of the tone of the comment. 'Crown for the Clown Office' was another headline, aimed at the Crown Office which heads the prosecution (or Procurator Fiscal) system in Scotland. It handles all prosecutions in the separate legal system of Scotland in the name of 'His Majesty's Advocate' (the Lord Advocate). The lawyer known as the Lord Advocate is a political appointee who also sits in the Cabinet of the Scottish Government. The current holder was known to be an SNP supporter but belonged to the opposite wing of the party to radicals like Sine Die. There was no love lost between the two wings.

Helen Dyer knew she was under pressure, especially from above in the Police Scotland hierarchy. There was no doubt in her mind that she had the perpetrators in custody but in the continued absence of the jewels and without a confession, she was up against it. She instructed Police Scotland Media Liaison officer to issue a statement saying that 'the enquiry was ongoing and no further comment would be forthcoming while suspects were in custody.'

She had a full day's work ahead of her, questioning the suspects and for most of it she was sitting across the table in the interview room with Musa Iqbal. Occasionally she would yield the lead role in the interview to one of her inspectors, and Musa would ask one of his junior colleagues to sit in the solicitor's chair, but by the end of the day they were both thoroughly fed up looking at one another, and Helen was becoming increasingly tetchy.

It would probably have been worse if the Sine Die members had decided to parrot 'no comment' to her questions but all three of the suspects were, on the surface, quite willing to answer questions and despite being interviewed separately, all sang suspiciously from the same hymn sheet. Usually there are small variations in the accounts of those who are telling the truth. Either this lot had rehearsed well or their story was true, which was unlikely. The video of their police interviews at this time showed them all admitting freely to being at the Castle but denying any involvement in carrying off the Honours.

The driver of the white van and his mate denied

they had anything to do with the theft and said they had been in Edinburgh on an evening out and had parked their van in the West End. They maintained their van was not the one seen in the Meadows and without the fake number plates the police had more work to do to connect them to the drone.

DCI Dyer therefore concentrated her questioning first on the three men who had been in the Castle. The one with a shaved head and clean shaven, was clearly the leader so she questioned him first. His name was Stewart McSween and he worked as an electrician in West Lothian.

DCI Dyer said: 'You don't deny you were trespassing in the Castle during the Tattoo? Your purpose was what in being there?'

'We were preparing to carry a banner onto the Esplanade during the final scene of the Tattoo but we didn't get a chance. Someone stopped us.'

'Who stopped you?'

'I don't know. A guy in uniform who said we were in the wrong line and held us back. I think he was suspicious.'

'Suspicious of you? Why would he be that?'

'I don't know. I guess he looked at our faces and saw that we didn't fit with soldiers of the Royal Thai Rifles.' He smirked at his own attempt at humour since the three men were all obviously Caucasian.

The three men had been identified by matching

the photographs taken of those leaving the castle with ones in the Special Branch file on Sine Die. The other two arrested at the same time as McSween had black hair and short beards. One, named Alastair (or Aly) Gibson worked as sous-chef in one of the big Edinburgh hotels. The other man from Dundee, Jimmy Mone aged forty-two, was unemployed.

The two men arrested with the white Renault van came from the West of Scotland. The red-haired one, Tam Tolan, had his own plumbing business in Clydebank to which the van was registered. The other man in the van, Lee Stevenson, had a Chinese mother and Scots father and spoke with a strong Glasgow accent. He lived in Oban and worked as an engineer on the ferries to the Scottish islands. He had been staying at Tolan's home in Clydebank when the police called to arrest him and had freely admitted being with Tolan and the van in Edinburgh.

These two men were also named in the Special Branch file on Sine Die and like two of the Castle trio were in their late twenties or early thirties. Some of the other names in the file were university or college students and three were lecturers. Special Branch reckoned that about four dozen people were members of the group, a third of of them female. DCI Dyer kept the file handy in case she wanted to reference names in her interviews and ploughed on. Once she had interviewed all of the men she tried an old trick of re-interviewing them over the same ground to see if they would contradict their earlier statements. She started again with McSween.

'When did you enter the Castle?'

'Earlier that evening when the bands were going in to get ready before the start of the performance.'

'And those uniforms you were wearing in the photographs, where did you get them?'

'We saw them in one of the changing rooms. And luckily they fitted. I suppose you'll be charging us with theft but we didn't intend to keep them.'

Iqbal intervened to say his clients would admit taking the uniforms if the other charges were dropped.

'You must be joking, Mr Iqbal,' DCI Dyer replied testily. 'You're asking me to believe that your clients just happened to be in the vicinity of the Castle to do their demo the very same night the Crown Room was broken into. And then by sheer coincidence a video appeared - clearly shot by the thieves - which claimed to be from the very organisation to which they belonged, espousing the very same view that was proclaimed on their banner - Scottish Independence.'

McSween butted in before the solicitor could speak. 'Actually the banner said 'Only a Fool likes London rule'. Nothing about independence but I'll make it easier for you, Chief Inspector, I won't deny we are campaigning for independence. Exactly what organisation are you alleging that we belong to? The SNP?'

'You know perfectly well, Mr McSween. It's called Sine Die or Syne Dye or however else you want to pronounce it.'

'I know there is such a group. In fact someone showed me yesterday's Daily Record and they seem to know all about it. But I'm not a member. In fact it's a secret society from what I gather. So how can you expect me to know about something that is a secret?'

'Because you and your mates meet at a church in Glen Clova which is owned by a Trust linked to Sine Die and you all happened to be in Edinburgh the same night the Crown Jewels were stolen. Do you deny that?'

'Well, I don't deny being in Edinburgh that night. I've already told you we came to make a protest at the Tattoo. My friends with the van were giving us a lift afterwards but they couldn't get parked and so they moved on to the West End. As for meeting in that church. No doubt you will have pictures of us meeting there, but that's not a crime. The Trust that owns the kirk is sympathetic and lets us use it. We meet to discuss independence and what we can do to further it. Because none of us live in the same area we meet on neutral ground. One fella lives in Oban, two in Glasgow, two in Dundee and I live in West

Lothian as you well know, so we meet PRIVATELY and we share our political thoughts which - of course - are none of your business unless this is now a police state. We share a dram, light a camp fire and bunk down for the night. If I had known the Deep State were taking an interest in us, I might have made a complaint. In fact I think I will.'

'There is no need to be facetious, Mr McSween.' Helen was inwardly fuming and fighting not to lose her temper, so she took a break and went back to her office. The interview was going nowhere and she knew it.

Just as she was preparing to resume the interview, an ace arrived in her hand. PPE suits and masks, similar to the type of Personal Protective Equipment worn by CSI and the police themselves at crime scenes, had been found the day after the theft stuffed into a rubbish bin in the upper castle area. When the thieves smashed the glass around the Honours, one CCTV camera had recorded them wearing such suits. The other camera which was fixed nearer head height had been blinded by one of the thieves who had sprayed it with car paint from an aerosol found with the discarded PPE.

DNA had been taken from the suits recovered from the bin. Matching it with the DNA samples taken from the three suspects would establish if they were indeed the culprits and prove their claim to have been present only in the lower castle area was a lie. The forensic tests had been fast-tracked and were back. The DCI studied them and let out a loud 'Yeeeeeees!!'. Her team all looked up from their desks. To her delight and theirs, the DNA traces in the suits and masks matched the DNA samples taken from the men after they were arrested. She made her way back to the interview room where Iqbal was waiting for her.

'Detective Chief Inspector, my clients have made a free and full explanation of why they were at the castle. I suggest that unless you have actual physical evidence linking them to the theft of the Honours, you release them today.'

'I'm sorry, Mr Iqbal, but I'm not prepared to do that.' Now that DCI Dyer had got the physical evidence to charge the five men she had in custody, with some satisfaction she declared, 'Your clients will be charged with theft, taken back to their cells and appear in court tomorrow. I think we're done for today.'

CHAPTER 9

Those who thought the men would be charged with something dramatic like terrorism or conspiracy would have been disappointed when the charge was simply 'theft'. Those with legal training might have wondered why charges were brought so quickly but with huge media and public interest in the case, there was pressure on the Fiscal service to bring charges. Besides, they and the police were sure they had the right people in custody. Having been made to look fools by the fake Honours in the kirk in the Angus Glens, they were determined to be seen to have made progress. The process of getting all the pieces of evidence together (what prosecutors call getting their 'ducks in a row') would last for a few weeks until the case came to trial.

The best thing Helen could hope for now was that she and her team would find the jewels and perhaps a bonus of fingerprints, or that one of the men would give up the hiding place in exchange for a lighter sentence. She conceded the latter was unlikely and she had no clues to the hiding place of the Honours. So her priority became finding the drone. An army unit which trains military personnel in using drones is based at Glencorse south west of Edinburgh and had reported that one of its drones had temporarily gone missing but was now back in place. She turned to her sergeant, DS Cameron Meiklejohn.

'Get out there, Cameron.' Make sure no one touches it until we get forensics to have a look. And when you talk to forensics ask them to hurry up with the results on that white van.'

While the interviews had been taking place, two other detectives on Helen's team had been trawling through the CCTV footage around the area the white Renault van with false number plates had last been seen. One of them, DC Natalie Barnes, was complaining she had square eyes and conjunctivitis. Helen already thought the girl was a 'flake' but agreed to let her take a break and turned to her colleague, DI Roderick Cairns, a smart graduate entrant to the police who was prone to offer suggestions when they were not asked for. She took the view it was better to have any new ideas than none.

'What have you got, Roddy? Any leads on the vanishing van?'

'Well, Ma'm, I think I may have identified where they switched the plates. When they left the Meadows they came through Tollcross, down Lothian Road. Now they had a choice of going left opposite the Usher Hall out the Western Approach Road, or continue right to the bottom where they had to turn right and go round the end of Princes

Street into South Charlotte Street and up into
Charlotte Square. Lots of cameras there and it's in
the new ULEZ. Except they didn't arrive there. So
they must have taken the Western Approach road
and turned right at the first set of lights into Canning
Street. There are a couple of places with not much
traffic in the service road at the back of the offices.
They could have swapped plates there out of CCTV
coverage and then gone back onto the Western
Approach Road and out west with the genuine
number plates. We picked them up at Wester Hailes
and then on the M8 as they carried on all the way to
Clydebank.'

'With the drone and the Honours still in
the back?' (At this point the police had not yet
interviewed the soldier from the drone depot who
later revealed the van stop in Canning Street had
been to hand him back his drone).

'Possibly.'

'But when we arrested the guy who owns the
van there was nothing in the back. So they must
have dropped off the contents between the Western
Approach Road and the guy's home in Clydebank.
Probably out of sight of any cameras.'

'There is one other possibility, Ma'm. When they
made a 'pit stop' to change plates perhaps they did it
next to another vehicle and off-loaded the drone and
the jewels there.'

'In which case it's a waste of time tracking the white van across the whole central belt to Clydebank.' Her irritation grew. 'No, it's not. We should do a timeline on the van and see if it could have stopped anywhere on the way to Clydebank. It could help to narrow down where the Honours are hidden. But let's hope they didn't stop for a pee and we end up searching a toilet. Tell DC Barnes to buy some Optrex and get back to work.'

'If I may, Ma'm? Should we also be looking through the list of Sine Die members that Special Branch gave us to see which of them have vehicles which might have been used for a potential swap or drop, or who live at places along the route.'

Helen Dyer knew he was right. She was tired and grumpy, having interviewed the Sine Die men for a whole day. DC Barnes moaning about her eyes had pushed her to react by doubling down on the CCTV search. She realised now the info on the other Sine Die members might also lead them somewhere.

'Good thinking, Roddy. Do it. And get DC Barnes to share the timeline on the van with you. If there are gaps and they coincide with places near to where members of the group live, we might get something.'

As expected, the 'Sine Die Five', the new sobriquet the tabloids had bestowed on them, got bail when they appeared in court the next day. They surrendered their passports and agreed to report to the police every week until the trial took place, normally within ten weeks. It meant that they could no longer be brought in for further questioning. In any case, it was unlikely they would say anything useful other than trot out the same explanation of being at the Castle for a protest stunt, hoping a not guilty plea would work.

Musa Iqbal got his moment in front of the cameras explaining that they would be pleading 'not guilty' since they had been unfortunate to be at the Castle at the same time the Honours were stolen, concluding, 'My clients do not deny being supporters of the independence movement but that does not make them thieves.'

He and Rosie were yet to be given the results of the DNA tests which they would need to be given as part of 'disclosure' process between defence and prosecution, and Helen Dyer was in no hurry to hand them over.

Chapter 10

The next development in the story was nothing short of sensational. However, it has remained unknown to everyone except a few insiders. Had a newspaper or blogger run a story saying that the King had met with Sine Die while they were awaiting trial, it would have been put down as a wild conspiracy theory. But that was what happened next.

King Charles had been as appalled as anyone when the Honours were stolen. Although they technically belonged to the Commissioners of the Regalia, it was HIS Crown and sceptre and he wanted them back. Sending a letter with the Royal Seal to Sine Die effectively saying 'Please can I have my jewels back' was not going to work. But Charles had shown that he was quite capable of intervening on affairs which were not directly political and he was determined to do something.

Each year - and it is every year, come rain, hail or Covid -The Royal family spend several weeks on the Balmoral Estate in Deeside in Scotland. This annual pilgrimage had begun in the time of Queen Victoria and had been embraced by subsequent Royal families. The monarch stays in Balmoral castle and there are other cottages and lodges which can be allocated to members of the Royal family. For the many years he was Prince of Wales, Charles had the use of Craigowan Lodge on the estate, giving him some privacy. When the royals are in residence, it is customary for the Prime Minister and spouse to spend one weekend at Balmoral, and most weekends a minister of the Church of Scotland is invited (without spouse). He or she preaches on the Sunday at Crathie Kirk with the Royal family in the pews. The absence of a clerical spouse is said to date from the time Queen Victoria had a crush on a minister named Norman MacLeod and the Queen did not want his wife around. The emphasis is on a mix of informality and ritual following the same pattern each weekend. Queen Elizabeth, who had enjoyed childhood summers at Balmoral, was especially fond of her time there. On Saturday evenings, her consort Prince Philip would light a barbecue at a spot in the countryside around the Castle, to which they all drove in Land Rovers.

At the time of the theft from Edinburgh Castle, King Charles and Queen Camilla were in residence at Balmoral and the king had been kept informed of progress (or rather lack of it) in the search for the Honours. He already knew about the raid on the church in Glen Clova which as the crow flies, is due south of Balmoral by only a few miles, and apparently laughed when he heard about the fake jewels.

There are no roads as such on the estate but forestry

tracks criss cross the heavily wooded hills which are part of the Cairngorms, from which the Angus Glens stretch southwards. When the conspirators of Sin Die had been meeting at the former kirk in the valley, they were physically close to the man whose crown they had stolen.

Charles decided this was a coincidence too good to pass up. He would meet them in total secrecy in the woods which lay between them and ask them to consider giving back the Honours. He would warn them that they could face stiff prison sentences, and having achieved what they wanted in the way of publicity they should simply hand the Honours back. Of course the King was conveniently ignoring the small matter of their demand for secession from the United Kingdom.

The King had learned from his briefing by Special Branch and by one of his Royal protection unit officers that Sine Die were not all die-hard republicans determined to do away with the monarch in an independent Scotland. They knew (whether they personally favoured the Monarchy or not) that this would not be popular and damage their cause. Charles was nothing if not a pragmatist and was, as his mother had been before him, on courteous terms with the leadership of the SNP government in Scotland. Official SNP policy was to retain the monarchy and if they got their way over independence, the Scottish Crown would be used to crown the monarch once again. That was the theory but he had learned long ago to be wary of promises from politicians.

The expression on the face of the King's secretary, Sir Alan Toby-Smith when Charles explained what he had in mind, would have been worthy of a cartoon. Eyes bulging, eyebrows raised, the Secretary began immediately to outline the downsides of the King's plan in the same manner that Sir Humphry, the Whitehall mandarin, used in the popular television comedy series when he knocked back one of the Prime Minister's bright ideas.

'First of all, Your Majesty, there is the danger that this group will refuse a meeting and someone will leak this to the media. That will result in endless negative comments about pandering to criminals, interfering in the judicial process et cetera et cetera. And just suppose they agree to a meeting, what happens if they then leak this to the media with the same negative result?' He paused and looked as if he was about to confess something. 'Or what happens, sire, if someone in the Royal household should leak this, where would that leave us? With the same result. After all it has happened before....'

The 'Palace' to the joy of the tabloids had often proved to leak like a sieve and they were prepared to pay a lot for information such as this.

'Well, Alan,' King Charles began. 'I have already

considered that. We - that's you and I - will do our utmost to keep this tight. We will ask for a solemn assurance from these chappies that they will keep it secret and if they don't, well I have already considered what I will do. You know the Palace motto has always been 'don't complain, never explain' when it comes to the media. But, if it leaks out that I met them, I will make a video like they do and I will explain to the nation that I would have been negligent in my duty if I had not done everything in my power to get back the Crown and the Jewels. Short of a Royal pardon, it's the least I can do.'

Sir Alan Toby-Smith looked as if he would have a fit at the words 'Royal pardon'.

'I'm not sure that would be wise, sir.'

'Well, like it or not I'm at least going to try. Now that they're out on bail where can we meet them? The police tell me they have a meeting place in a disused church over the hill in Glen Clova. Halfway between there and here would be around Loch Muick and it's on our land. It would be jolly private unless they bring a camera in a drone...sorry Alan, only joking. There's that little boathouse where we could meet them. Just one thing. I don't want their lawyer there - that Iqbal creature. Can't stand him. Always showboating about something. He's not bringing his showboat on my Loch!' The king laughed and Sir Alan paled. 'One more thing. Let's make it even tighter by inviting only the ring-leader. Chappie called Stewart McSween my sources tell me. Please set the wheels going, Alan.

Sir Alan knew he was being given a task with huge potential to go horribly wrong but he loyally set about it. The trusted Royal protection squad detective inspector Ted 'Chalky' White was dispatched to Edinburgh. DCI Dyer and her team were not informed and kept out of the picture. Accompanied by a Special Branch detective, DI Atkinson, he went to the home of Stewart McSween. The two men showed their credentials and asked if they might have a word in private. McSween had just arrived home from work but the policemen already knew this since he was the object of discreet surveillance as were his fellow accused. His employer had been sympathetic by allowing him to continue working while out on bail.

'Am I being arrested?' McSween immediately asked.

'No, sir, you are not. We have something to discuss with you which is very much in your interests but we cannot do so here. Would it be possible for you to come with us?'

McSween looked understandably suspicious. Could this be a trick by the Deep State to eliminate him? Such things were the stuff of thrillers he had read. He said nothing.

The Royal detective tried another tack.

'We promise to have you back in a few hours and apologise about the short notice. We can't compel you to come with us but again I urge you to come as it will be of great advantage to you if you do so.' McSween was intrigued. The man had asked politely and there was nothing threatening in his manner.

'Can I bring my phone? It's got a tracker. I want my wife to know where I am.'

To McSween's surprise the man agreed. 'Yes, that would be fine.'

The two policemen had discussed this possibility and agreed that when they got to Glen Clova, mobile signals would be temporarily jammed around the area. In addition, in case McSween used his phone to record anything or take pictures he would be asked to leave the phone behind when they took a Land Rover through the forestry tracks to Loch Muick. In less than two hours after they left McSween's home they were driving into Glen Clova. Twice on the way the police driver had used the blue lights with which the unmarked police car was fitted to make sure they sliced through early evening traffic.

During the drive Stewart McSween had relaxed enough to make conversation about football with the two detectives. He was a Hearts supporter and DI Atkinson, the Special Branch man, followed Celtic, so it made for a diversion from the business in hand. Neither Sine Die nor the Honours were mentioned. The policemen did not disclose anything further about the purpose of the trip but when they by-passed Forfar on the A90, McSween asked, 'So it's the kirk in Glen Clova, is it?'

'You'll see,' Atkinson replied. When they turned into Glen Clova, it was not the church building they headed for but the Forestry centre. A muddy Land Rover Defender was already parked there. 'We'll need to take this for the next section,' DI White explained. 'The road from now on is not exactly motorway. Our driver will wait here and we'll be back in an hour. Please leave your phone in the car.'

McSween immediately became suspicious again. His body tensed. Were they going to kill him in the forest and hide his body? Or make it look as if he had committed suicide?

As if they knew what he was thinking, the Special Branch man said, 'Don't worry, you're safe with us. You've been reading too many thrillers. Suppose I told you that you were going to meet the King, would you believe me then? Probably not, but that's what you are about to do, sunshine. First we need you to promise that what goes on for the next hour remains totally secret. If you don't give us that promise, witnessed by DI White here, the deal's off and we all go back to Livingstone and it's your word against three of us that it ever happened. OK?'

McSween hesitated, then said, thinking they were not being serious, 'Yes, I readily promise that I will not tell anyone I met the King.' He could still not believe the policeman was not joking and so there was no harm in giving the men the promise they wanted.

They got into the Defender and bumped their way up a forest track until Loch Muick came into view. It was dusk, or as the Scots call it, the 'gloaming'. Their vehicle pulled up at a boathouse on the shore of the Loch. As they got out, a familiar figure emerged from inside the boathouse and said in unmistakeable tones that have been mimicked countless times. 'Good evening. Mr McSween, I presume?'

Now aware that he was indeed meeting the King, Stewart McSween experienced an emotion that was rare for him with his confident can-do personality - awe. King Charles was used to the effect he sometimes had on people and even militant nationalists can wobble when they are caught unawares. The King continued, 'Thank you for coming, I appreciate it.'

As if I had a choice, McSween thought to himself. Then, recovering a little of his customary confidence he replied, 'I'm not sure why I'm here, sir.' He remembered someone saying when you meet the monarch you should address him as 'Your Majesty' in the first place but he was not going to play that game. 'Sir' was as far as he would go.

'I apologise for all the cloak and dagger,' the King continued. 'But it is necessary that this meeting remains private - and by that I mean totally confidential. Not a sniff to the media. I understand you have already given that undertaking. Yes?'

'Ye-es,' said McSween but it came out in a stutter.

'I think you now understand how the media can pillory people. 'Tartan terrorist', for example. I imagine you like that as much as I like the stuff they call me. Shall we walk, it's more private that way?' The king set off along the path skirting the large Loch and Stewart McSween fell in alongside.

'Please don't tell me that you didn't take the Honours, Mr McSween. I know you did but you're not here to plead guilty or otherwise. Besides even if you did tell me you took them, no one can hear us and it would not be admissible. But there is something I want to ask you right at the outset. Are you and your group Republicans? In other words, if you get your independence, are you going to get rid of me?'

McSween hesitated. 'Well some of our group are republicans but most of us are proud of the role that kings played in the Nation's history. If we have universal voting, parliamentary democracy and a constitutional monarchy in Scotland, then there is no reason to get rid of you, sir. We would stay in the Commonwealth. And of course the European Union.' He smiled as he said the final part.

'Well, no problem with that,' replied the King. 'I needed to know because it affects how I phrase my next remark. If you were going to abolish the monarchy, then taking the Honours would be simple theft with overtones of blackmail or a ransom demand but I know you don't like it being called that. I saw your video. But if you want the British monarch to remain King of Scots and the Prince of Wales as 'Duke of Rothesay', then, in a way we're on the same side. They are OUR Honours.'

McSween looked puzzled. 'What is it you want?'

'I want you to return them. Gesture of goodwill and all that. Remember those chappies who took the Stone of Scone - no, of course you don't – you weren't born then. I was just a 'bairn' myself.' The King grinned as he pronounced the word with a Scots accent. 'You know what happened to them? Nothing happened to them. They had made their point and got their share of limelight. It worked and no one suffered. Now you could do the same. Pop them in the post or leave them in a ruined Abbey or some such thing and everyone will be happy.'

'I think you're forgetting, sir, that we are about to be put on trial. How do we know we will be given credit for returning the Honours?'

'You're right. I forgot you have already been charged, but what if you do a 'plea bargain'? The Yanks are always dealing them out in their courts. By the way, you will notice I'm not asking you to tell me where you hid the regalia. If you did I could become 'an accessory after the fact', I think they call it. Unless of course I shopped you. But I give you my word this meeting is our secret and what we say remains here. So what do you say, Stewart?'

The use of McSween's first name was the King's way of keeping up the charm offensive. The two men had circled back and were approaching the boathouse.

'I'll certainly think about it, sir, but as you can imagine it is not my decision alone. I will put it to the Sine Die members – of course I will not say it came from you.' Both men laughed.

'You can pretend it came from a ghost. Hamlet's father was a King, was he not?'

'I don't fancy myself as Hamlet. In any case, that play ended in a bloodbath.'

They both laughed again and shook hands and as McSween got back into the Defender, the King said quietly but audibly, 'Bloody clever that operation in the Castle. In wartime it would have got you all a medal.'

As Stewart McSween rode back later in the unmarked police car, his companions were no doubt curious what he and the King had been laughing about but he did not tell them anything. He was too preoccupied with what he would say to his fellow conspirators. What if they wanted to keep the Honours hidden? Or worse, if some did and others favoured a deal with the prosecution, it could undermine their solidarity. He also realised they would need to consult their solicitor and their counsel before the trial.

CHAPTER 11

The next few days brought challenges for everyone involved in the Honours saga.

Sir Alan nervously scanned the newspapers and social media, fearful that the meeting at Loch Muick had been leaked. If the King's initiative in meeting the leader of Sine Die should become known he did not relish the criticism which would inevitably be levelled at the King from all quarters (including the legal establishment). It would lay him open to the charge of interfering in a legal case. Notwithstanding this, the King remained confident his action would be seen as a reasonable attempt to do everything he could to recover the Crown Jewels.

So far, nothing had leaked from the Royal side.

For his part, Stewart McSween kept his word and did not tell even his wife what had happened at Loch Muick. She might think he was going potty and having delusions. He told her the police had wanted him to open the Sine Die church and search it again in his presence. He needed now to bring together the five accused and discuss the King's suggestion without saying where it came from. He did not want the responsibility for himself alone. Realising that if they were to give up the Honours and change their plea, they would need to involve their solicitor. He called Musa Iqbal who told him that Rosamunde Michelle had already asked to meet all of the accused and had proposed a location in which they would have privacy. It was near to Haymarket which was convenient for the men travelling from Dundee and Glasgow. McSween agreed and Iqbal promised to call him back with the place and time.

DCI Helen Dyer was having a better day. Her ducks were almost in a row. The results of the DNA from the PPE suits was so far her most powerful piece of evidence. Her team had got a little further on tracing the journey of the white Renault van. The CCTV timeline on the van had determined it made a short pause around Canning Street before it resumed travelling away from the City centre on the Western Approach Road. Then another pause out of camera coverage in the Murrayfield area before it had gone out by Wester Hailes, joined the M8 and continued non-stop on its way back to Clydebank. The officers concluded that Canning Street and Murrayfield were the places where the van had regained its legitimate number plates and off-loaded the drone and the jewels. It was progress and was soon to be supplemented by another development, a result in the hunt for the drone.

The drone which had been reported missing from the army storage depot was back in its rightful place but when its temporary disappearance was investigated, suspicion fell on a known nationalist sympathiser who worked at the depot and was adept at flying drones. Unfortunately for him, a routine check after he had gone off duty on the Friday in question had found one drone unaccounted for and that was how they caught him. The drone in question was quite capable of handling a pay-load sufficient to carry the Honours out of the upper castle and down to the Meadows. This soldier was questioned under caution and had been offered leniency if he gave up the names of those who had recruited him to fly the drone.

So far he had admitted that some 'mates' he had met in a pub who had heard him lamenting about cuts to the army, had paid him to assist them in a prank to fly the drone up to the Castle and down again under the cover of the noise from the fireworks at the end of the Tattoo. They had told him they wanted to smuggle a banner protesting army cuts which their accomplices inside the Castle intended to hang from the castle walls. He had no idea, he maintained, what had come back down with the drone in a black sack. He admitted he had been operating the drone in the back of the Renault van parked near the Meadows and when the operation was over, the two men had returned him to his own van parked in a side street off Canning Street, a quiet spot at that time of night. They had off-loaded the drone to his vehicle and then drove off onto the Western Approach Road. He said he had taken the drone back to the depot the following day.

* * *

Rosie's plan to meet Musa Iqbal's five clients prior to the trial date being set, was an unusual one. Between her flat in Eglinton Crescent and Glencairn Crescent opposite, is a private garden surrounded by railings. Its gates are accessible only to key holders (the proprietors in the two Crescents). These gardens are an oasis of calm in the West End, enclosing an acre of lawn surrounded by trees and shrubs. There is a small playground for children at the east end but the garden at the other end is usually empty. It was five minutes walk from Haymarket railway station and thus convenient for all those travelling into Edinburgh as well as Rosie herself.

She suggested 6pm as the time for the meeting so that any onlooker seeing the group would think it was just a social gathering. She had engaged me (Max) as a waiter to serve drinks to the group from a folding table and chairs she had borrowed from downstairs neighbours. Those present consisted of the five accused; Rosie and her junior (an advocate who supports a KC when they appear in a higher court); plus Iqbal and his two junior solicitor colleagues who had come through from Glasgow.

Rosie began by welcoming her guests and introducing herself and her junior, Marco Nardini.

'I wanted to make this a friendly occasion to get to know each other because we will soon have to begin the hard work of preparing for trial. Here we have some privacy, and to dispel the image Glaswegians have of Edinburgh people, that they never offer hospitality, Max, who is a friend of mine, will be over at the drinks table out of earshot to top up your glass when necessary. Musa tells me that so far you have been all of one mind. You want to enter pleas of 'not guilty' and that was how I saw it too. But there have been developments in the past two days which I am going to ask Mr Iqbal to outline. These have come to us through disclosure by the Crown and we need to consider how they affect our case. Musa.'

Iqbal gave out the news about the DNA results on the PPE suits and the arrest of the army guy who had supplied the drone. He went on, 'These two developments make the case against us more dangerous. We can still maintain that the security footage at the Castle has nothing to do with us but how do we explain that your DNA matches with the discarded PPE suits? Then there is this guy with the drone. We can't pretend that he doesn't know you, Aly, because you both are regulars at the pub near the hotel kitchen where you work. We checked him out. If he says he did it for a lark (or even that you paid him) and didn't know what it was all about, it still leaves us having to explain what was in the black bag the drone brought down. It's all heavyweight evidence for the prosecution.'

Stewart McSween spoke first. 'What if we own up to taking the stuff and give it back on the eve of the trial, could that not work well in our favour? Assuming of course we stole it in the first place.' He grinned mischievously as he said it. 'What do you think, Rosamunde?'

Before she could answer, Tam Tolan jumped in. Known as Big Tam, he was the driver of the Renault van which belonged to his plumbing business in Clydebank. 'If we cop a plea do we all need to do it? I mean if Lee and I said we drove my van and did the drone thing for a prank. They can't pin the jewels on anybody without the actual stuff, can they?'

Rosie answered him. 'I don't think that will work. Whatever was in the sack was still coming out of the Castle and the pressure will be on you to say what you did with it. If you all admit the crime it would be easy for me to put a strong plea for a suspended sentence. Assuming of course that you did it.' She flashed McSween a smile. 'But it's got to be all of you. Otherwise you need to get different counsel for each different plea. And perhaps even different solicitors.

I'm not telling you what to do, just finding out what Musa and I need to do.'

Tam spoke again. 'I vote we cop a plea and tell them where to find the stuff. Ma business is on the line for this. I've got a good mate who's covering but what if they don't release my van and I go to jail. Ma business will gang doon the Clyde.'

'Can we talk about this on our own as Sine Die?' McSween interjected. 'Privately I mean. Now. We don't have time to have a meeting before we go back home or go up to the Glen. We need to decide today.'

He guided his pals over to a spot next to the bushes at the edge of the gardens. I had not heard any of the dialogue up to this point. Having unwisely taken an aperitif myself, I was bursting for a pee. The options were to desert my post and go up to Rosie's flat or nip into the bushes. The Sine Die men had not noticed that there was no one behind the drinks table. In fact I was in the bushes right next to where they were now standing and I heard everything of the ensuing dialogue.

Jimmy Mone made the first contribution in his broad Dundee accent.'Whit's it gonna be then? Ane fur 'a and 'a fur ane? Isnae that whit the Musketeers say?'

'Aye, Jimmy it would be good if we are all in agreement,' McSween answered. As possible prison terms were at stake, this was his chance as leader to hint at what the King had suggested. 'I have it on good authority that if they get the crown and jewels back when we go to trial, we'll no' be seen as villains and we may even get off with a fine.'

'Good authority' wha's that? Oor brief, Musa?' Tam Tolan was speaking again. 'We 'a ken he's in it for the publicity, but at least he's guid at his joab. Ah vote we cop a plea.'

Stewart McSween responded. 'No, Tam. It wasn't Musa. It was a bit higher up the tree. But I agree with you. What do the rest of you say? What about you, Lee? You've been silent so far.' He turned to the man with a Chinese mother, 'Confucius, what he say?'

'I'm for pleading guilty and asking for mercy. I have been suspended from my job. As a ship's engineer I can get another one working at sea but this Oban run suits me fine and if we don't have to do jail time, I might keep it. But maybe we should wait to spring it on them at the start of the trial. Maximum impact.'

'Agreed', said two of the others. No one else objected and it was soon unanimous. Sleepless with worry since their arrest, the realisation that they could find themselves in prison, had preyed on the men's minds especially those with families to consider. The chutzpah they had felt when planning and carrying out the crime had evaporated to be replaced by relief at seeing a possible escape route offered to them.

Jimmy Mone, the Dundonian, then made a comment in his local tongue which astonished me if I had understood him correctly. He asked, 'Dae we aktually ken whar the jools are, lads?'

Lee Stevenson answered him. 'Tam and I gave the drone back to the wee army guy and we dropped the black bag at that Sub-Post office on the way hame as Stewart telt us. But surely it's no still there.'

'It's OK, Lee,' said McSween. 'It's somewhere safe. Our friend at the Murraygreen Post Office is not sitting on it. We have had too many centuries of the English sitting their bums on our Coronation stone. We've stuck a suppository up their depository. That's all I'm saying for now. We agreed at the start that we should keep the final hiding place to only one of us, and you chose me. The Post Office guy also knows where the bag is but he doesn't know what's in it. It was best for him not to know if we were caught. Rest assured it's in a safe place. So shall we tell our voluptuous advocate what we've decided?'

They walked back over to where Rosie and Iqbal were in earnest conversation. I stole back to my barman's post. It said something for McSween's leadership that they were happy to trust him with the hiding place, and it did make sense that the fewer who knew the place the better.

As the unofficial leader, McSween spoke for the

rest. 'We are all agreed to give the stuff back and change to guilty pleas but only when the trial starts. It hopefully will be counted in our favour. We trust you, Rosamunda, to do a great job in keeping us out of prison.'

Rosie beamed. 'I'll do my best and it will definitely help if you give the jewels back. In the light of the discovery evidence, I must say I think you've made the right decision. Let's hope next time you come to drinks in this garden I'll have a good reason to open a bottle of champagne.'

One of the five, I forget which, fancied themselves as a wag. 'Was that fizzy water you gave us no' champagne then?'

The question went unanswered as Iqbal's team shepherded the men to the exit gates and hurried themselves to get the next Glasgow train.

'Catch you on Zoom tomorrow, Rosie,' shouted Iqbal as he ran after his colleagues.

She turned to her junior counsel. 'Well, Marco, at last we know which direction we are going in. I have a feeling this is heading for a happy ending but let's not get ahead of ourselves in case they don't cough up the Honours.'

Marco Nardini helped me carry the table and chairs into Rosie's neighbour's basement flat and went off to catch his bus. Since the introduction of Ulez to Edinburgh and the city's punitive parking

charges, cars became a liability and the excellent
Lothian bus service is now as quick and much
cheaper than a taxi. Rosie brought the remaining
bottles and I carried a box of glasses up to her flat
where we polished off the remaining Prosecco.

'You happy?' I asked her. 'I couldn't help hearing
that last bit.'

'Yes, mostly. As long as they keep their word and
give up the stuff, I reckon I can get them a suspended
sentence and perhaps a fine for the damage to the
Crown Room. They'll easily pay for that with crowd
funding. There are a lot of people out there who
see them as heroes.' She paused. 'Thanks for your
help. You know that you can't repeat anything you
may have overheard out there. Also it's good to have
someone with whom I can share at least part of the
pressure. Normally that would have been Helen but
obviously in this case that's a no-no.'

At this point I should have told Rosie what I had
overheard in the bushes and should have shared my
astonishment that apparently only one of the five
(plus someone in a Post Office) knew the actual
location of the jewels. Looking back I know I should
have told her there and then, and by not doing so
I suffered for this later, putting our relationship in
jeopardy, but somehow it did not seem the right
moment. I wanted to seize the opportunity to steer
the conversation away from the legal case to more

personal matters.

'Talking of trust, I saw your desk diary open when I was waiting for you the other day, and I started to count the days since we first met, or rather had dinner together. In a fortnight it will be a hundred days. Can we do something special? My contract at the university is about to end and I want to go out in style.'

'Of course we can. That would be lovely, Max. But what are you going to do? Are you giving up history? You can't go on living in that poky haunted flat. You could stay here but somehow I don't see you as a kept man.'

'And I won't be. I have the proceeds of a previous house sale invested and I intend to change direction. As a graduate already, I could take an Ll.B in two years and perhaps study to be a solicitor. What do you think?'

'I don't think. It's you who must think if that's what you really want to do. But being a solicitor is even more boring than medieval history and the big firms have stopped hiring. Too many lawyers. Let's talk about the options more. Perhaps when we go away for our hundred days celebration?'

'It's a deal. I do have a little job coming up. I'm writing an article for the Sunday Mail on all the places in Scotland where Sine Die might have hidden the Honours. The places are all based on history and all very patriotic, like the ones we speculated about the other night with Helen. Like Arbroath Abbey or that wee kirk in Kinneff where the women hid the jewels. Or Bannockburn or the Wallace monument. I reckon these Sine Die guys are more romantics than terrorists and they'll choose somewhere symbolic.'

'I'm surprised a newspaper is not running a book on where the Jewels are hidden. You know, 10/1 on Bannockburn, 5/1 on the Wallace monument. Another newspaper has offered a reward but it doesn't look as if Stewart McSween's ready to claim it. Frankly I hope I can trust him to cough up the jewels. There was too much bravado in that video for my liking …Until we are.. a nation again'. She sang it. We are a nation, that's what these romantic buggers don't get. But I'm a jobbing actress and I'll do the biz. They're not the first clients I disapproved of.'

'Do you mind if I ask you something? I hope you don't think I am prying but when I looked at your diary I noticed that every month for the past six you have written 'Longforgan'. Is that a place or a person?'

Her face darkened. I feared the worst but was wrong.

'I should have told you before now. I have a son. I was a wild child in my teens and got myself pregnant. My parents were very anti-abortion on religious grounds. They said they would support me but only if I had my child adopted. Of course you don't know what happens to the child after that but he or she in later life is entitled to find their mother. And my son did. A year ago. It has not been easy. At first it was all happy endings but it turned out to be the beginning of a guilt trip. God knows I felt guilty enough at the time but I got over that. After all I had NOT aborted and my son had a new life with parents who doted on him. I was not suited to be a parent, then or now. But what I did not expect was that after a lot of sweet talk he would try to make me feel guilty for giving him up. That was too much and so unfair.'

'Does he not have a good life in Longforgan?'

'Good life!' she scoffed. 'He's in prison at Longforgan, soon to be released. I don't know what to do. He's got my gift of the gab. It helped me to become a successful advocate but he has used it to con people out of money and to make me feel I'm a bad person. At least he didn't ask me to defend him in court. He only got in touch after his sentencing and said he needed me to help him sort himself out. Sorry, you don't deserve to get this dumped on you.'

'I do. Burden shared and all that.'

'Thanks. But there's not much you can do. You can't change the past.'

'It's not about the past, It's about the future. Yours – and maybe mine. I want to meet him if you'll let me.'

She relented. 'All right. Next visit to Longforgan you can tag along.' She then told me about some of the scams and cons which had landed her son in prison. We hugged silently before going to bed.

After Rosie went off to work next day at Parliament House, before heading off to Glasgow to deliver my article to the Sunday Mail I did some research. HMP Castle Huntly in Longforgan is Scotland's only open prison with the capacity to hold 284 low supervision adult male prisoners from various Local Authority areas. Its internet entry states:

Following a robust risk management process and a period in closed conditions, prisoners can progress to Castle Huntly where the emphasis is on careful preparation for release.

I was looking forward to accompanying Rosie there, but less so to the emotional complications that might accompany his release.

CHAPTER 12

The Sunday Mail paid me generously for my article and even gave me lunch at Rogano restaurant. I suspect the Features Editor saw me as a good excuse to have a nice lunch on expenses. I had written articles for newspapers previously but never for a 'red top' or tabloid. The truth is that it's much more difficult than writing for the Telegraph or the Guardian. Short words and sentences are required with the kind of striking sharp slogans that would fit on a placard at a demonstration. At the time I did not know that my article would never see the light of day and be overtaken by events which I set in motion.

It came about this way. I had taken the train to Glasgow and on the return journey as my train was approaching Haymarket station I had a Eureka moment. I noticed a substantial red brick building with the large letters 'Jenners Depository' above it. (Jenners, the up-market store in Princes Street had been Edinburgh's answer to Harrods but was now no more, after an epidemic of store closures in city centres, although the sign itself had been listed under conservation regulations and so had been retained). However, the building itself was still a storage facility for individuals and businesses known now as

'Edinburgh Storage'. I had considered using it when I moved back to the city a few months ago, because transferring my belongings to my attic flat would have been impractical. In the end I had left them in a friend's barn in Essex.

The area in which the building is situated is known as Balgreen and Tam Tolan had said something about handing the black bag to a man in a Post Office.

But it was the large sign on the building that triggered my memory of what McSween had said to his mates while I was listening in the bushes in Eglinton Crescent gardens: 'We've stuck a suppository in their depository' or words like it. Where would it be more natural and secure to hide treasure than in a storage facility? By using the word 'suppository' McSween was making a crude joke. He was saying 'We put it up 'em' in the immortal words of Private Jones from Dad's Army.

I ran up the stairs at Haymarket station, turned left to the tram stop and quickly bought a ticket. A tram was just leaving for the airport. I jumped on and took it to the Balgreen stop, the first after Murrayfield Stadium. Round the corner was the entrance to the Edinburgh Storage facility on Balgreen Road. I went to the reception and said I was thinking of leaving something valuable.

'This may seem a silly question, but do you have

CCTV?'

'No it's not silly,' replied the charming lady at the counter. 'All comings and goings of clients are recorded on video and saved on the cloud. Not of course the contents of the storage units.'

That was all that I wanted to hear. 'Thank you. I'll be back in touch.'

I ran out on to Balgreen Road and walked around until I found what my phone had told me should be there, Murraygreen Post Office. Like many sub Post offices it doubled as a corner store and I looked at the newspapers on the stand. The Edinburgh Evening News had just arrived and as it was late afternoon, most of the morning papers were missing. I bought The National, the newspaper most sympathetic to the SNP. I asked the man behind the counter who wore a turban if he sold many copies.

'Unfortunately no,' he said. 'People around here vote SNP but they don't want independence. You may look at me and say 'He's not Scottish. He won't want independence', but I do. My family comes originally from Punjab. There we know all about independence or rather the lack of it. So now I am Scottish I fight for Scottish Independence and we Sikhs know how to fight!' He grinned.

His wife came from the back shop and interrupted. 'Vajarit, I told you no politics at the counter. You will lose us customers.'

'But all the customers agree with me,' the man replied.

'That's because all the ones who don't agree have stopped coming here.' She turned to me. 'Ever since that terrible Post Office scandal with the faulty software and so many innocent post masters wrongly accused of theft, my husband has been campaigning for Scotland independence.' she added, as if the Post Office scandal was a valid reason for supporting independence for Scotland.

'I hope you were not one of those wrongly accused,' I said hoping to get more information from the Post Office proprietor. It was looking more and more likely that as the drop-off point for the black bag on the night of the theft.

'Actually,' the woman replied. 'We were lucky. We got this Post office because the poor man who had it before us was convicted falsely. Wrongly. And we know others who were put in court.'

Her presence had made her husband less talkative so I took my leave and went back to the tram stop and opened my copy of The National, which was full of stories linked to the theft of the Honours. The letters page was 50-50 on whether Sine Die had dealt a blow to the independence cause or given it a much-needed boost. By now I was buzzing with the thought I might be able to tell the police where to recover the Crown Jewels.

I called Police Scotland on my mobile and said I had an urgent message for DCI Dyer. To my delight I discovered her team was based at Gayfield Square Station, directly on the route my tram was taking. When I called them, I asked to speak to DCI Dyer urgently. After a minute wait, Helen came on the line.

'This had better be good, Max. If you are bearing a white flag from Rosie she doesn't need to bother. I've already forgiven her. Like me, she has a living to earn.'

'No, it's nothing to do with Rosie. It's to do with the case. I have come into some important information. I think I know where the thieves have hidden the Honours. I need to see you. Please.'

Helen Dyer, I knew, would not be happy with me interfering in her case. I didn't know if Rosie would be either but I was determined to get my theory checked out and the more I thought about it the more it made sense. In any case, she could not afford to ignore my information.

'All right. You can come here. I'll tell the desk.'

In twenty minutes I was ushered into DCI Dyer's office. Helen was behind her desk and gestured to a seat opposite.

'OK, Max, let's have it. By the way, does Rosie know you're here?'

'No. I didn't want to compromise her. She doesn't

know about this information.'

'Just exactly how did you come into possession of this information you have?'

I explained about the meeting in the garden and how I had overheard McSween talking to his mates separately, away from the lawyers. I was just about to say how I had realised his comment about a suppository was a clue to the whereabouts of the jewels when she brutally interrupted me.

'Stop right there, Max. I'm about to do you a favour by throwing you out. You can come back later with Rosie, if she'll let you. What you are telling me is that you were present at a meeting between counsel, a solicitor and five clients, acting as a wine waiter and eavesdropped on the accused. The meeting was privileged and if Rosie learns that you breached that, then her clients could sue her silly and she would be reported to the bar. Did you think about that?'

'No,' I replied sheepishly. 'I thought it was my duty to tell the police where the jewels are being hidden...It was entirely accidental me overhearing them. I thought if I told Rosie she might get into trouble with her clients or you.'

'But as Rosie's dumb waiter you had no business interfering. I know about you playing detective in Paris last year. She told me. Now, I could if I wished, milk you dry for your info, act on it and come up a heroine. That's if you're right. But you will have endangered Rosie's career and she will be rightly pissed off with you. If you're wrong and I waste my time on your theory, then I will be rightly pissed off with you too. That would make two of us pissed off with you. I'm telling you this because Rosie was - and is - a good friend of mine.'

The pissed off remark reminded me why I had been hiding in the bushes but continuing to excuse my eavesdropping as accidental and unintentional seemed pathetic, so I stayed silent and took my bollocking.

'What you maybe don't know, Max – I'll give you the benefit of the doubt here - is that there are strict rules that the police, the solicitors and the fiscal plus counsel on both sides have to follow in a case like this. There can be no underhand stuff or overhand-of-God stuff á la Maradonna to get the ball in the net, or it's a mistrial. Then it's red cards all round. Rosie meant for the best in having that meeting in the garden no doubt but it has backfired on her. You need to put that right by going to her with your theory and let her deal with it. As an officer of the court she is bound to come to me or the Crown office if she acquires information pertinent to the enquiry. It's called disclosure. That's why we had to tell Iqbal and her about the DNA match from the PPE suits and the fact that the wee army man has coughed to letting them play with his drone. So off you go and see what Rosie says.'

I mumbled thanks, and took a taxi to Rosie's. It was now early evening and thankfully she was in. I explained what had happened in the garden and how I had deduced the hiding place. She listened stony faced as I told her about checking out the Depository and the Post Office. I was sure she was angry at me and from what Helen had said, she had good reason. Feeling guilty for not having told her right away, I then massaged the truth a little by saying that I had called Helen to ask her advice about what to do with my info.

'And Helen told you to come to me,' she said breaking her silence. 'That was good of her. She could have destroyed my career. You both could.' That last remark hurt.

'I'm very sorry, Rosie. I didn't think. I got carried away when I thought I had solved the mystery. Surely it's important to get the jewels back. Your clients are going to plead guilty anyway and it will help them to get leniency if the jewels are back where they belong.'

'Yes, but that is none of your business. Don't you realise that there is a big difference between the police being led to the jewels by you, and my clients volunteering to tell the police where they are hidden. My clients won't be very pleased if they have had that option taken away from them. It's an important part of my being able to get leniency for them. And if they learn that you got that info by eavesdropping at a meeting I organised with them, they will be mightily angry at me. And rightly so. Why did you not tell me this right away?'

'Because as you say, it was your meeting and you would have been blamed. I wanted to keep you out of it. After all it was an accident that I overheard the conversation...'

'Of course I would have been blamed. But I'm not going to waste time on being angry with you. I need to do something about this right now.'

'I'm really sorry, Rosie. I acted rashly and stupidly. Can I simply stay out of it now, say nothing to anybody and hope McSween tells the court where the jewels are when he pleads guilty.'

'No you can't. You would be withholding critical information from the police. Now that I know, so would I. The key to it now is that McSween tells them where he hid the stuff. If he decides not to, he will be a damn fool. It would be like saying 'You know I took them, find them if you can'. Very unwise. But there's another issue here which can't wait. Now that you have told Helen about what you heard, she can't un-hear it either.' She drew a deep breath. 'OK, here's what we'll do. You will drive me to Livingstone to McSween's home. We will set off immediately. This will have to be done tonight.'

During the half hour drive she said very little and my stomach was churning so much that I nearly missed the Livingstone off-ramp on the M8.

'Max, you will wait in the car unless I call you while I explain the options to Stewart McSween.'

'Options?'

'Yes, there is a choice here. I will tell him that you have come into possession of information about where the jewels are being hidden. You may be able to stay out of it. I hope so. If I have to bring you in to speak to him you should not tell him that you got this info while you were waggling your willie in the bushes. That will reflect badly on you and on me. Let's hope he doesn't guess. I will then explain that if this information is correct he must tell the police now where to find the jewels and we go ahead as planned with the leniency plea. That is how I will begin. The alternative is that I will resile myself from the case and you share your info with the police. No, we share the info because strictly speaking now that you have told me your theory, I am duty bound to tell the police. Naturally I hope it does not come to that.'

'What about Musa Iqbal? Will he continue to represent the men whatever they choose?'

'I'm pretty sure he will. I'll call him tonight. It's me who will get it in the neck if anyone learns you overheard a conversation among the accused during the course of a private (essentially privileged) meeting. As my invitee you became part of the meeting.' I winced again.

'Is there any way I can protect you? I love you and I'm so sorry.'

She did not react to my declaration of love or my offer to help, and I knew I had hurt her badly by my impetuous actions. We pulled up at the McSween home and she got out of the car, slamming the door behind her and went inside.

Rosie's talent in persuading juries was now focussed on one man. She began by telling him that she had come into possession of information about the hiding place of the Jewels.

'If that information is correct, Stewart, then I am duty bound to take it to the police and they discover the jewels. That will take away the advantage you and your colleagues would have in making the disclosure when we go to trial.'

'None of my lads will have squealed. Only two people know anyway. One of them is me and the other one has not been arrested so he's not going to give himself away.'

'Sometimes people don't know when they give things away.' She paused and looked at him keenly. 'I want to ask you directly - are the Honours in the Jenners Depository? Taken there by the Postmaster in Murraygreen?'

There was a stunned silence. Rosie could tell by the look on Stewart McSween's face that she had hit the bull's eye. He gasped.

'How do you know?'

'Never mind how I know. You and your mates didn't tell me. They didn't know anyway, as you've just told me. Musa Iqbal didn't know. The important thing now is what we do. If you tell the police before they find out, then we'll get a good press before the trial. Now it's my duty as your counsel to say that if you don't want to give the stuff up yet, I have to resile myself. I can't go on representing you in court knowing this and not passing it on to the police. I'm sorry.'

'Don't be. All the lads agreed in the meeting we had in the garden that we didn't want to go to jail and we would have to give up the jewels anyway before the trial. Might as well be now as then. But I want to leave the guy at Murraygreen out of it. He might have guessed when I was arrested what was in the sack but he did not know anything that night when it was handed to him. It wasn't put in his deposit box but the one in my wife's name which I paid for. Vijarit's had a rough deal with the law over the post office scandal. His cousin owned the Post Office before him and he took it over when the cousin was charged. He doesn't deserve this. I will take the police to the storage place myself and leave him out of it. I have the key and the code.'

'May I also suggest you make a public statement through Musa. He's good at these. I'll do the necessary for a plea of mitigation at the trial. Do we have a deal?'

'Sure,' McSween agreed. 'I'm sure the others will be OK with this. I'll phone them tonight. We've no option now. But please stay on as our lawyer. It would not look good if you quit on us now.'

Rosie put out her hand and patted him on the arm. 'I'll call Musa Iqbal and DCI Dyer tonight and she'll probably call for you in the morning. Best of luck, and thanks for seeing sense.'

Rosie came out to the car and told me in two words: 'All good.' As we drove away she took out her mobile and started explaining the new development to Iqbal and Helen Dyer. I had dropped out of the picture and huge relief swept over me. I also knew that by getting herself out of a tricky situation professionally she had also saved me and perhaps saved our relationship

CHAPTER 13

DCI Helen Dyer picked up Stewart McSween first thing the next morning and took him in a police car to Edinburgh Storage. Her team had been up early, and had already obtained a warrant from a judge to look at the CCTV in the Storage facility. It showed Vajarit the sub-Postmaster entering the storage building on the morning after the theft, carrying a black cloth bag. Apparently he was a regular and had his own locker, as well as the one rented for his friends in the Sine Die movement in McSween's wife's maiden name. McSween gave the police a statement declaring that Vajarit never knew what he was asked to put in the storage locker and had never asked. The postmaster repeated the same story and the police and procurator fiscal told Vajarit Singh they did not intend to pursue the matter.

With the Honours back in custody, Musa Iqbal summoned a news conference and announced that the accused had given back the Honours and were changing their plea, inviting clemency from the court. The Sine Die Five stood behind him. As accused persons awaiting trial, they could not speak publicly at this stage.

As for Rosie and Helen, they opened a bottle of

champagne at the Eglinton Crescent flat and to my intense relief, invited me round to share it, but not before giving me a hard time.

'You know, Max, now that you are giving up history, you could always get a job as a detective' said Rosie.

'Aye,' Helen put in, 'You could do surveillance in the bushes with your willie hanging' out but then again we might arrest you.'

I pretended to find this funny but I was still ashamed of my actions. More importantly I was genuinely glad the two pals were back together now that the case was over. The Sunday Mail did not of course run my article given the new developments but they let me keep the fee. When Helen left us she took a taxi, as we had consumed two bottles between the three of us.

There was still the trial to come. At first it looked as if public opinion would pressure the Crown into dropping the charges but there was also a substantial lobby against letting Sine Die get off scot free. It was argued their actions could encourage other militants. For that same reason a number of stiff sentences had been handed out recently as a deterrent to Just Stop Oil protesters in England.

I attended when the case eventually came to the High Court in Edinburgh, Lord Kerrigan presiding. There was no need for a jury as the accused had all pleaded guilty, but the circumstances of the theft at the Castle had to be outlined in order for them to be properly sentenced. The police evidence was outlined by DCI Helen Dyer who was led through the results of her team's investigations by the prosecuting fiscal, Advocate Depute (AD) Laurence Rennie KC.

As the accused had already admitted being at the castle and taking the Honours away by drone, to the relief of Special Branch it had not proved necessary to detail how the photo IDs taken at the castle had been linked to their thick files on Sine Die. That Branch of the Police Force do not like publicity for their officers, and do their work mostly in secret. It would have meant acknowledging surveillance of private citizens who had committed no crime. Rosie had agreed to this. Any rocking of the boat at this point would not have gone in her favour.

In her evidence Helen referred to the DNA on the PPE suits, the CCTV tracing the van in the Meadows and its brief stop to offload the drone in Canning Street before carrying on to Murraygreen and returning to Clydebank. The original police interviews in which the men denied taking the Honours were replaced by new statements they made after their change of plea, in which the accused confessed to the crime and making the YouTube video. Tolan and Stevenson also admitted dropping the black sack containing the Crown Jewels at the flat occupied by the Singhs above the Murraygreen post office. Reference to the fakes discovered in the church in Glen Clova was tactfully omitted by Helen.

At one point during DCI Dyer's evidence Lord Kerrigan intervened to ask:

'The proceeds of the theft, the Honours, were in the black sack given to the sub-postmaster at Murraygreen who then deposited it in Edinburgh Self Storage. Why is this gentleman not among the accused this morning?'

'I can answer that M' Lord,' said AD Rennie. 'On investigation we were assured by the accused and by Mr Singh himself that he was entirely unaware of the contents of the sack. It was deposited by him as a favour requested by the accused Mr McSween because the facility is closed at night and he was at work the next day. The self-storage unit was in the maiden name of Mrs McSween and the accused paid the storage costs. We therefore deemed it unnecessary to bring charges given that all the stolen property has now been returned undamaged to the Commissioners of the Regalia.'

The judge still looked dissatisfied. 'I might want to hear it from him myself. But for now I have another question. In the evidence DCI Dyer has just given, she spoke of a drone used in the theft. Where did this drone come from? Who operated it? And why is he or she not in my court this morning?'

Advocate Depute Rennie looked uncomfortable as he answered. 'The police have established that it came from an army depot at Glencorse. It was operated by a serving member of the armed forces who did so apparently thinking it was just a prank being played by the accused to hang a banner from the Castle walls. He has given us a statement to this effect, as have the accused who assured us he did not know what the drone was carrying when it returned from the Castle.' The AD cleared his throat, 'We have decided not to bring charges since he is being put before a court martial by the army for his role in taking the drone and operating it without proper authorisation.'

'Very well, proceed,' the judge responded. To the relief of both sides, the postmaster was not called by the judge who seemed to want to wrap up the case as quickly as possible.

DCI Dyer finished her evidence by detailing the original arrest of the five men and told how McSween had come forward with his solicitor to say they now wished to change their plea and had taken her to the Storage facility where they had recovered the Honours. The judge congratulated her on a job well done and called on Rosamunde Michelle for the defence.

Rosie called character witnesses on behalf of the men: the employer of McSween in the electrical contractor firm for which he worked, and the manager of the hotel kitchen where Aly Gibson worked as a sous-chef. The skipper of the ferry on which Lee Stevenson worked, and the partner of Tolan in the plumbing business in Clydebank both gave glowing testimonials to them as reliable and honest men. The SNP Member of Parliament in Dundee stood as a character witness for the unemployed Jimmy Mone who had helped as a volunteer in his constituency office. None of the men had a prison record and this was their first offence of any kind.

When Rosamunde Michelle KC stood to give her plea in mitigation in her wig and gown, she looked gorgeous (to me at least, and I suspect I was not alone). She began by saying the case had aroused a lot of interest and there was considerable public support for the men.

'Part of that support can be explained by the fact that a substantial section of the public share the political opinions of the five accused. They are unashamed Scottish nationalists who want independence for our nation. That is not itself a crime and it is a widespread aspiration as our election results show. But we have a democratic system of government to decide such matters and that is the lawful way to go about achieving change. The accused were mistaken and misguided in the actions they took. But this case is not about politics, it is about a romantic dream; it is about five men frustrated perhaps in the political sphere who have taken action to draw attention to their vision. Yes, the Honours of Scotland were taken but they have been returned unharmed. What we are dealing with is, m'Lord, not political activism or even terrorism, as some of the less sympathetic Media have described it. We are dealing with Romantics and their dream of an independent Scotland.

The Honours of Scotland have at times in our history been put aside and forgotten, but they remain a symbol, a potent one, of our sovereignty. By taking them these five men wished to draw attention to their aspirations. They would be better described as Romantic Rogues who love their country, not thieves. They are decent hard working men as you have heard from their employers and colleagues. Nor are they trying to undermine the Democratic system. They simply chose a different, albeit illegal, way of attracting public attention to their dream. You may see them as misguided or foolish but their sincerity is not in doubt. They have demonstrated it by their willingness to restore the Honours to the proper authorities and they are willing to make good the damage done to the Crown Room. There was no one harmed physically, no funds stolen and no other people were compromised or harmed. They concede that they are guilty as charged but were foolish and ask for the mercy of the court.'

'There is a precedent for a theft of this magnitude of symbols of state: it is the case of the Stone of Scone, the Coronation stone taken from Westminster Abbey in 1950. In that case no custodial sentence resulted, no charges were brought and the matter has passed into the national consciousness as a reminder of our distinguished history as a Nation in Scotland. You might even argue that it resulted in greater sensitivity towards the way the Stone is used for ceremonial occasions. Perhaps the outcome of this case will help the nation to appreciate the Honours more than it did in the past when they were left forgotten for over a century in a walled chamber until Sir Walter Scott and compatriots rescued them. We may not share my lord the political opinions of the men in the dock but we cannot doubt their love of their country. I ask you to consider clemency in sentencing them today.'

Lord Kerrigan announced he would reserve sentence until the following day and court was adjourned. I don't know whether the judge consulted anyone overnight in government or elsewhere but he came back with a very short judgment. Perhaps he did not want it picked apart by anyone on either side of the political question of Independence. He accepted, he said, the sincerity of the men although they had been misguided in their way of pursuing their dream, and he would take into account the fact that they had made restitution of the Honours before they came to trial and that they were willing to contribute to the cost of refurbishing the Crown room. However, he could not on any account overlook the priceless nature of the objects stolen and the waste of police time. There was also the question that their actions could encourage others to commit similar acts.

He then gave four of them a suspended sentence of four years each and a sentence of six years to Stewart McSween, also suspended. The suspensions meant that should any of the men commit further breaches of the law they would go to jail. It was as much as Rosie could have hoped for. She, the men themselves, and Iqbal and his team were all relieved.

The five men were shepherded out by Iqbal to meet the media. I waited for Rosie outside court to congratulate her but she had already gone off to lunch with her junior. I texted instead.

Our relationship was still fragile and I knew I would have to prove worthy of her trust. That evening I arrived at her flat with a bunch of red roses. A week later we celebrated with a weekend at Cromlix, Sir Andy Murray's hotel near Dunblane. I dared to mention the word 'Longforgan' again and with relief learned that I was still welcome to accompany her when she paid her next visit there.

THE END

To Kill a
Crimewriter

Chapter i

Most people know that the patriarch of detective fiction, Sir Arthur Conan Doyle, was born in Edinburgh, where he later qualified as a doctor. He moved to the south coast of England where he turned to writing crime fiction and created Sherlock Holmes. What is less known is that four leading contemporary crime writers also live in the city of Edinburgh at the present time. They are all very different in character, as are the detectives who are the heroes of their stories. Two are men and two women, and their books have sold millions worldwide.

They were guests of honour at the unveiling of a long-overdue monument to Conan Doyle in his native city. All four would be the target of an attempted murder in the days to follow and the person planning the crimes was also a guest at the dinner. As was I.

My name is Max Quillan, until recently a medieval historian, but that career is now history and I am currently looking for a new role in life. While I decide what to do, I am temporarily a Trustee and live-in janitor at the Sir Arthur Conan Doyle Centre in the West End of the city, occupying a grace and favour attic room on the promises. The building was once the home of a brewery baron and Sir Arthur never lived there but the Centre's promotion of matters psychic would have gladdened his heart. I was lucky to be representing it at the event in the absence abroad of the Founder and the illness of the Chairman of the Trustees.

The other guests had been chosen to represent aspects of Conan Doyle's interests and passions: These included spiritualism of course which he embraced in later life, but for me there were some surprises: the military (he got his knighthood for patriotic dispatches in the Boer War), and his range of sporting interests. The police were also represented, as was the Judiciary, perhaps a nod to that part of ACD's life when he successfully overturned miscarriages of justice. It was not difficult to find people who admired ACD but so diverse were his life and interests that it had been decided to invite only those who lived in the city of his birth.

The event had been organised by the Royal College of Physicians whose President had conceived the idea of celebrating the great writer and had raised the funds. The dinner was held in the magnificent RCP building in Queen Street.

Prior to the meal we gathered a hundred metres east along Queen Street in the Scottish National Portrait Gallery where we were in for a surprise. Many had assumed that the monument to Sir Arthur would take the form of a new portrait, a bust or statue which would be unveiled. Most of the existing portraits show him dressed like a country squire, smiling through his croissant moustache.

There are plenty of portraits of ACD in London but none in the Scottish National Portrait Gallery. Or would the 'monument' take the form of a statue? It is ironic that the only statue celebrating the great man in his native city is outside his birth place at the east end of Queen Street, but it is of Sherlock Holmes. The idea of a new way of celebrating Doyle in Edinburgh was that of RCP President, Sir James Keillor, a well-liked figure and an amateur magician like ACD's one-time friend Houdini. I wondered what he would conjure up. Perhaps a death mask like the ones in the first floor gallery where Voltaire's is on exhibition alongside those of notorious murderers.

As we gathered in the magnificent ground floor vestibule of the Portrait Gallery, glasses of sparkling wine in our hands, Sir James, a tall figure with a narrow nose and high cheekbones who reminded me of Peter Cushing, welcomed us and spoke of his own passion for the writings of Arthur Conan Doyle. He then introduced a young man with a wispy beard whose hair was gathered into a bun on his head. His name was Nikita Trifonov, not a painter or a sculptor but an AI adept and the creator of what we were about to see. The lights dimmed and suddenly on the far side of the space Sir Arthur Conan Doyle himself appeared as a life-size hologram and began to speak in his distinctive Scottish brogue.

'As you know I believe that at death we are all reconstructed in some non-material form. I am very happy to appear here in the twenty first century to remind you that this is possible and especially to be doing so a few hundred yards from where I was born. Thank you for coming.'

It was as eerily effective as the ABBA experience in London which I had seen a year ago, and for a moment most of us thought we were looking at a living being, not an avatar. A couple of ladies clapped a hand to their mouth as if to prevent themselves crying out in shock.

The image disappeared and a stunned silence reigned until someone began to applaud and we all joined in. Sir James pointed to Nikita who looked sheepish and nodded in appreciation. He explained he had used AI to put together 'Sir Arthur' from recordings, film and photographs. The best bit for me was the voice, so eerily close to the clips of the man I had seen on film although the words had been written by Sir James Keillor in line with Sir Arthur's own beliefs.

Although the whole enterprise had been Sir James' idea, it had been embraced enthusiastically by the Director of the National Portrait Gallery, Lucrezia Gaudie, who welcomed us briefly and explained that we were the first members of the public to see the display. She tactfully omitted to mention that those who had donated funds for the equipment and Nikita's fee had already seen the display the previous evening. The media, she said, would be invited to view it the following day and a place would be found in the gallery where it could be shown to the public on a permanent basis.

The show over, we walked the hundred metres to the Royal College of Physicians' hall buzzing with excitement and approval of the way that AI technology had been utilised for a museum exhibit to bring Sir Arthur back from the dead.

The Lord Provost had tagged along to the dinner to say what an asset to the city the 'monument' would be. Someone whispered to me (I forget who) that he had probably never read any Conan Doyle but wanted to meet the celebrity writers who rarely appeared together. Our host Sir James Keillor, President of the RCP, stood up and went round the room explaining which aspect of ACD's varied life each guest represented, apologising that it had been necessary to limit the number of guests as the Appeal funds to pay for our dinner left after the costs of the AI exhibit would not permit a larger occasion.

The splendour of the room, surrounded by portraits of medical 'greats' was lavish enough for me, and the menu card (which listed the attendees and which aspects of |ACD's life they represented) looked delicious: Seared scallops with hollandaise sauce; Aberdeen Angus Beef Wellington; Dumfriesshire cheeses and Cranachan (a concoction of roasted oatmeal, whisky, raspberries and cream).

The room was set with five circular tables covered with white linen on which silver cutlery and candlesticks shimmered under the crystal candelabras. At the top table in one corner of the room the four celebrity writers were seated with Sir James, plus Lucrezia Gaudie and the Lord Provost. It was the only one with a microphone. A place had been set for Nikita as well but he didn't show up. At first I thought this might be because he was casually dressed at the unveiling ceremony while the rest of us were in black tie mode but apparently his partner was due to give birth and he was sitting in the labour ward at the hospital.

The other four tables could be roughly categorised as: university and medicine; legal and police; literary and publishing; sport and other interests. I qualified under the last category, as did the chair of the spiritualist church which meets in our building. He turned out to be the CEO of a big property agency and had been a Trustee of the ACD centre (as was I now), but chose to address me as if I was the janitor (which I also was by virtue of occupying the tiny servant flat in the attic).

Our table was certainly as diverse as the interests of ACD himself. The boxing representative was in fact a promoter and not an active pugilist. The cricketer and the golfer were long past their playing days and were both from the world of high finance. They conversed a great deal about rugby which holds no interest for me at all. Bashing heads and thumping bodies has never appealed to me as sport as it is distinctly unhealthy. As is war, but military personnel are usually very sociable and I adopted Basil Fawlty's advice not to mention war to the colonel from the Castle sitting next to me. He remembered my role in recovering the Honours of Scotland the previous year and we got on well. The man who sat on the other side of me had plenty of interesting facts about ACD and his holidays in Switzerland where he had introduced the Swiss to cross country skiing which he had learned in Norway. Now retired from a post in the Cairngorms, he lamented sadly that climate change was putting paid to the Scottish ski resorts.

The other two places at my table were taken by an urbane Edinburgh publisher and the lady who runs the Book Festival whom I thought to be rather pleased with herself. The latter two knew each other well and conversed about people and things of which I knew nothing. Since I knew no one else in the room, I longed to be at the legal and police table where my lady friend Rosamunde Michelle KC, a criminal advocate, was representing the Scottish bar. She knew Sir James well. He had been the best pal of her former partner with whom she still had cordial relations (hence the invitation direct to her). Rosie had also managed to wangle that the police invitation went to her best friend, the feisty DCI Helen Dyer with whom she had been at school in Currie. Looking around I could see what a tight-knit society Edinburgh still was.

The dinner was delicious, the wine plentiful and the speeches were short. I would have welcomed hearing more from the four celebrity writers who were each invited to speak for five minutes on what they appreciated about Sir Arthur. First up was Florence Scott Thomas, better known as F.S. Thomas, famed for her sci-fi books for children but read by adults worldwide. The success of her books and the movies based on them had made her famous and very rich. She uses her wealth in philanthropic ways but that had not saved her from internet trolls when she criticised the actions of several protest groups. Since then she had been forced to employ personal security at her home in south Edinburgh.

Looking for new challenges, she had used a pen-name to reinvent herself as a crime writer for a series of books which had proved immensely successful even before the author's real identity was revealed. She was currently working on the seventh book and a television series had propelled her pseudonymous crime writer into the top ten in the UK. Ms Scott Thomas spoke of her appreciation of Conan Doyle's early struggles as a writer and how he had invented so much of the forensic approach to crime that we now take for granted.

Next to speak was Anton Ross whose books are based in Edinburgh and whose detective is an unorthodox policeman much attracted to alcohol. The son of a West Lothian miner, Anton Ross often chose the villains in his books to be the great and good of Edinburgh society by whom he was surrounded as he spoke. Eschewing the temptation to point this out, he praised Conan Doyle's invention of Sherlock as a kind of anti-hero and his somewhat love-hate attitude towards the police.

The next speaker was Caitlin Mossiman, born in Liverpool whose convent school education had filtered out any Scouse tones. Her accent was mercifully free of talking about her work as 'wherek'. She had studied Eng Literature at St Andrews where she had met some weird people who later featured entertainingly in her books. She observed that the Dr Jekyll/Mr Hyde theme and the other dark 'shadow' characters found in the work of RL Stevenson and James Hogg were echoed by Conan Doyle in Sherlock and Professor Moriarty. Although her books featured a Scots detective, there was less police procedure in them and more oddball behaviour. In her five-minute tribute to ACD she stressed his ability to bring weird and wonderful people and plots into his stories rather than the cliches of the country house mysteries and upper class murders involving inheritance which were the backdrop to so many detective books in the so-called Golden Age of detective fiction in the 1920s.

Last to speak was the quintessential Edinburgh New Town Man. Ronald MacKenzie was a qualified physician, now a hugely successful writer whose hobby was playing in a jazz band. He had written two series of books celebrating the quirks of Edinburgh middle-class life of which the public could not (to my bewilderment) get enough but by far his crowning achievement which had brought him international success, was his creation of an Asian woman detective who plied her trade in the streets and alleys of Hong Kong prior to 1997.

His support for the Dalai Lama had led to his books being banned in China. As a former physician, for him the hero of the Holmes stories was Doctor Watson and he had the audience laughing loudly when he read out instances when Watson treated people who had been gassed, concussed and ill-treated by prescribing simply a large brandy. He also made the serious point that ACD had a strong passion for justice as his work in righting the miscarriages of justice in the cases of George Edelgee and Oscar Slater.

All of the Big Four authors had spoken warmly and wittily about Sir Arthur and what a splendid memorial the hologram was. They also knew the value of keeping to the time they had been allocated and it was only a few minutes past ten when everyone emerged from the RCP building, still talking about the innovative avatar. As I was leaving with Rosie she said she had forgotten the menu which she wanted to keep as a souvenir of a memorable evening but had left hers on her table. I volunteered to go back into the Royal College to get one but when I entered the dining hall, the catering staff had already cleared the tables. As they pulled off the linen cloth on the table opposite the one at which I had been sitting, I spotted a menu lying underneath it, ducked down and rescued it.

Rosie and Helen Dyer were standing on the wide pavement outside the College beside a police car whose blue lights were flashing. 'My carriage,' explained Helen, as I handed the rescued menu to Rosie. 'I'm on early duty tomorrow and as I'm here officially I get the perk of a car to take me home. Want a lift?'

We had already agreed that Rosie and I would go back for a night-cap to her flat in Eglinton Crescent where I intended to ask for one of Dr Watson's magic brandies. I lived around the corner in Palmerston Place and on the nights I stayed over at Rosie's I usually left early in the morning to assume my janitor duties at the ACD by opening up and check the heating. As the police car pulled away, Helen could not resist a tease.

'Ever been in the back of a police car before, Max?' I guessed what was coming. 'I had in mind to arrest you for obstructing the police over that business with the Crown Jewels, but Rosie put in a good defence, so I relented.' In fact Rosie had also been annoyed with me for different reasons but I knew both women had forgiven me. After all it was me who had led the police to the hiding place of the Regalia. 'Never mind,' Helen smiled as she delivered her punch line. 'They also serve who stand in the way.'

We were already turning left at the traffic lights opposite the ACD Centre so I smiled and didn't reply.

A minute later we were relaxing with our drinks in the soft leather armchairs in the bay window of Rosie's drawing room, she with a malt and I with an Armagnac. The curtains were open, the trees in the gardens were silhouetted by the moon and all was quiet save for the occasional taxi rushing past in the street below. I asked Rosie to get out the menu which listed the guests at the dinner, to find out who they were.

'I really enjoyed the evening but I didn't know anybody there except for you and Helen. What about you?'

'Well, I knew everyone at my table obviously and James Keillor whom I tapped for my invitation. I also knew who the people were at the table opposite you.' She frowned as if they were not to her taste. 'But the highlight for me was meeting the writers. They are all very different but charming in their own way. Florence Scott Thomas is a star but does not act like one. Ronnie MacKenzie is a charming in a very upper-class way. I think of him as straight out of Downton Abbey. Anton Ross is really nice, not a bit like his boozy boorish detective. Hasn't let his huge success go to his head and supports a lot of charities. Down to earth or should I say, under the earth given his father went down the mines.' She went on, 'Caitlin Mossiman was a bit less readable. She lives in Heriot Row next to one of my colleagues who is on the Bench. He said she says hello in passing, but keeps very much to herself. She has a big dog that she walks in Queen Street Gardens opposite her flat. I got the feeling she was taking me in, studying me. Perhaps I will appear in her next book.'

'As the vamp who gets the gangsters off the hook?'

'You can talk. The medieval man who finds shrouds and jewels wherever he goes.'

'Correction. Former medieval man now seeking employment.'

I wanted to talk seriously to Rosie about what I

should do now that my locum post at Edinburgh University had come to an end but now was not the moment and I was not sure that our fledgling relationship was yet firm enough to go there. So I reached for the menu I had recovered and started reading out the names at the table which had caused her to frown. 'You said you know some of these people at the table opposite mine.'

'Well, I know one of them personally, alas. Sir Martin Forbes-Graham. He's a forensic psychiatrist and visiting professor in the law faculty. Did a lot of work at Carstairs with the criminally insane. He's a patronising bastard when he gets into the witness box. Reminds me of that character played by Ian Richardson in 'House of cards'. He's married to Lady Louise Loudon KC, the Human Rights lawyer who sits in the House of Lords and is always appearing on radio and television whingeing about something. She's a cross between Cherie Blair and Helena Kennedy and spends most of her time in London while he stays in Edinburgh. He's also a letch.'

'Oh, you have evidence?'

'Not only that, experience. He invited me to dinner in the New Club after a case I had in which he gave evidence. At the time I didn't know he was married. Over dinner he was marginally less patronising than he had been in the witness box. Insisted on walking me home afterwards. He had just bought one of these new town houses at the back of the old Donaldson School building and said it was on his way home. Which I suppose was true. When we got to my door he seemed to think that he should have been invited in, and when I said thank you and goodnight, he got peevish. Dinner at the New Club is not a ticket into my bed and the kind of things he was saying bordered on sleazy. Two days later I got a pompous letter which would have been funny if it wasn't so insulting. Not a nice man.'

'And the others who were at that table?'

'The chief police surgeon who's a good guy. He and I have spoken many times in court. Then there was a GP from Liberton where ACD grew up. A very nice lady who told me she loved crime fiction and was thrilled to meet the Big Four. The other two I only know by reputation so I'm going to have to be bitchy again.'

'Bitch away.'

'Well one is a Reader in Criminology at the University of Edinburgh called Jason Dunnet. Fancies himself as an expert on crime but James only found out too late after he had issued his invitation, that he actually despises crime writers. He's a leftie who wrote a book on criminology but couldn't find a publisher so there may be a bit of green cheese there. Funnily enough he's also an active member of the Green Party and behind his back they call him 'The

Green Queen'. Once a year he gives a lecture to his students titled 'The crime of crime writing' in which he lambasts leading crime writers for what he calls their ignorance and lack of imagination. One year his students wrote on the lecture room whiteboard 'Whodunnit? Jason Dunnet!'

'Wow. I hope none of the celebrity guests got wind of his opinions or they might have pulled out. How did he get on the guest list?'

'Someone at the University had put his name forward (probably he did it himself) and he is the type to make a fuss if it was withdrawn. James told me he had a strategy to keep the celebrity guests from meeting Dunnet at the Gallery. After that we were all seated at separate tables, and the celebrities, if you remember, were ushered out first at the end of the dinner.'

'How appalling. The Judas at the feast...'

'I know you think James invited people who were part of his circle of friends like me. I might as well tell you now that I put in a word for Helen to get the police invitation, and suggested the ACD Centre got an invite when I knew you were able to take it up. The Dunnet guy was just a mistake, accepting the University nominee without checking. But Adrian Frei - the other person at the table - more or less twisted James' arm personally to let him attend. He is a doyen of the Book Festival and is the literary editor of Sunday Times Scotland where he writes a controversial column. Another failed crime writer, who is forced to self-publish his work. His letterhead displays his degree with (Oxon) after it, and he is constantly referring to Oxford University people in his conversation. Because of his portly figure he is known as the 'Oxon Cube'. Acquiring an invitation was a mild form of blackmail on his part. He promised James he would write up the occasion favourably and probably would have taken revenge in his weekly newspaper column had he been excluded. You will notice that he was seated at a different table from the publishing/writing group which included the Book Festival lady because they can't stand each other. It flattered him to be at the University table but it also kept the two of them apart.'

' Well, James must be relieved it all went off so well.'

'Indeed. He told me confidentially that the dinner was actually conceived to stage an event involving the four famous writers. The main idea was to get publicity for the 'unveiling' and that was guaranteed because the Big Four were there together. You probably saw there was a film crew at the Gallery, filming the hologram. They also filmed the dinner speeches for a television documentary being made about the hologram/avatar to get maximum publicity for it, in addition to the usual media circus tomorrow morning. Instead of us lot, James could have had all the donors to a dinner but some of them were insistent on being anonymous and not being filmed. So we were the stand-ins. The authors had a time limit on their speeches so they would not need to be edited and clips of their speeches will also be made available for TV news.'

I smiled at the detail in her gossip about the guests, and the brilliant way Sir James Keillor had brought off the event: keeping the donors happy and keeping the toxic guests apart as well as providing an audience for the celebrities who would bring maximum publicity. 'Thanks, Rosie, but maybe just as well I didn't know all that before the event. Would have taken away the feeling of a being a VIP.'

I looked down at the menu I had recovered from the floor. All the people attending had been listed. On the copy I had, against the names of the four famous writers little symbols had been drawn in pen, each one different. I assumed they were doodles and thought nothing more about it. It was not until two days later that the sinister meaning of the symbols became clear. We went to bed and 'Dr Watson's cure' ensured I slept soundly.

CHAPTER 2

Between the Royal College of Physicians building in Queen Street and Heriot Row in the New Town, are Queen Street Gardens, a large grassed area surrounded by trees and bushes, split into two sections by a street running northwards downhill. While incessant traffic runs along Queen Street, behind the garden railings is an oasis in the city centre open to keyholders from surrounding properties. Unlike many of the gardens in the West End where Rosie has her flat, dogs are permitted in the gardens. Every morning and evening Caitlin Mossiman emerges from her flat in Heriot Row and enters the gardens with Jasper, her black Labrador. She usually lets the dog off the lead which I think is against the rules but tonight there is no one there to see or complain. It is two days since the ACD celebration dinner. She is later than usual and it is already dark. The street lights of Queen Street usually provide some illumination but there are parts of the gardens planted with bushes which are in deep shadow and the black Labrador is scarcely visible as it runs ahead.

Caitlin Mossiman is dressed in the white raincoat in which she appears on the cover of many of her books. Tonight a headscarf covers her head and shoulders since there is a fine drizzle in the air. The scarf is secured around her neck by a large brooch, part of her extensive collection of costume jewellery. That is what saves her life. As she passes the shadow of a large bush a masked man emerges carrying a long knife. He rushes towards her and stabs her in the chest but the knife does not penetrate because it bounces back from the brooch. By the time the man raises his arm to stab again, Jasper realises that his mistress is being attacked and leaps to seize the man's arm in his jaws. The assailant drops the knife, shakes off Jasper and flees, exiting through a gate into Queen Street and running east toward the bus station in Saint Andrews Square. It is less than five minutes since she left her flat. They might have been her last minutes on earth but she is alive.

The blow has pushed the author back in to a sitting position on the ground where she sits stunned, unable to pursue her attacker. Jasper enthusiastically licks her face and she cuddles him close before taking out her mobile phone and dialling the emergency number for the police.

CHAPTER 3

The attack on Caitlin Mossiman was too late for the next day's newspapers, but not for Breakfast television which was soon running crawlers on its screens. 'Knife attack on leading woman writer in central Edinburgh'. It was soon trending on Twitter(X). For many there was only one leading author who lived in Edinburgh and that was Florence Scott Thomas who had already been the subject of trolling and death threats after her criticism of damage done by several protest groups in furthering their cause. Never ones to let truth get in the way of a good rant, the twitterati had decided the victim must be F.S. Thomas. And so began a wave of false trolling with some inevitably hiding behind their cowardly anonymity to declare she had got what she deserved. The writer, who lives in the suburbs with her family under her married name of Richards, was forced to issue statements on the medium she had long forsaken, to say that not only was she alive and well but she had not been walking her non-existent dog. Cue disappointment in tabloid newsrooms where they were gearing up for a story echoing the attack on author Salman Rushdie, replacing the villainous jihadist attacker with an eco-warrior.

After being checked in hospital and given some cream for the nasty bruise on her chest, and a pill to help her sleep, the writer had gone home in a police car, grateful that there was not a posse of reporters outside her home. Although her photograph was on the back cover of many editions of her books, she had had a hair colour change recently and her face did not appear often in newspapers or on television. She was a handsome woman in her seventies, now with a little more flesh around the jowls.

If her hair was worn down (as it was at present), it seemed to alter the shape of her face and made her look younger and more cherubic. It was not well known that she was a resident of Edinburgh but when her identity as the victim of the knife attack became public, she would need more than a change of hairstyle to guard her privacy.

DCI Helen Dyer was one who came to her door the next morning, accompanied by the junior in her team, detective constable Natalie Barnes. After the preliminary politeness had been gone through, it became apparent that both the author and Helen Dyer were plain speaking women which made the interview easier for both of them. The writer seemed more worried about Jasper being on his own after the attack than she was about the fact she had nearly lost her life.

'You live on your own, Ms Mossiman, I

understand. Have you had any threatening messages?'

'No, Chief Inspector, I can't say I have had any death threats or any weirdos sending me stuff. The weirdos I usually keep as characters in my books. The nasty things that have been posted about my books are water off a scouser's back. In any case it shows they actually read it. It's when nobody cares about your work that you need to worry.'

Helen Dyer was actually a fan, and had read several of Mossiman's books. She had lobbied her senior officer to get the case when it came up at the morning meeting. Little did she realise she would be opening a can of worms.

'Have you ever encountered any strange characters when you walked your dog previously? Is it always the same gardens?'

'Well, no ... and no. This was the first time I met someone other than a fellow dog owner and most of us know each other by now. I use the Queen Street gardens at night because it is right across the road from my front door. Easier and quicker and I'm lazy. But during the day I sometimes go down through the New Town and go along the Water of Leith walkway. He – that's Jasper – likes it there. The only problem it goes for miles in both directions and he can't resist a splash in the water.'

Hearing his name and the word 'walkway', the dog

began to wag his tail in anticipation. 'No, Jasper,' said the writer, her Liverpudlian origins more evident talking to the dog than in normal speech. She turned to the policewomen. 'I think this must have been someone who thought he could take advantage of a woman on her own in the dark. I don't think he singled me out.'

'Well, we don't know that. Needless to say we will have discreet patrols in both east and west gardens after dark for at least a week. If he's a nutter maybe he'll try again and we'll catch him. You live alone you said earlier? Do you have secure locks and a spy hole in the door? You're on street level but there's a basement flat beneath you. Is there access from the rear?'

'No. The basement flat (or 'garden flat' as the posh people of Edinburgh call it) used to be connected to this one, but it's blocked off. The locks plural are pretty good on the door into my flat. You come in via the street door and there's a camera above the buzzer. I don't let people into the vestibule unless I know them or am expecting a delivery. Even then I take a peek through the peephole before I open, always with the chain on.'

'Very sensible. Have you had any trouble in the past? Celebrity stalkers? Unwelcome mail or messages?'

'Not really. I don't count myself a 'celebrity'. A

few years ago I got some funny phone calls. Heavy breathing. It turned out to be a sicko who tried numbers until he got a woman's voice. So I don't think it was me he was after. Besides, I now don't even have a landline. I use a mobile with two SIM cards. Only my close friends know my personal number and if I don't recognise the incoming number on the other SIM, I let it go to voicemail.' She broke off. 'You know this whole thing is a real bugger. I've just started a new book and I want to keep working on it. I think I should maybe get away for a few days. There's a cottage I can use in the Yorkshire Dales... and I can take Jasper.'

'Do you think that's wise?' DCI Dyer interrupted. 'This attack could be random or it could have been targeted; we just don't know. Until someone is in custody it might be better if you were not alone in the Dales in a cottage. I hesitate to remind you, but for that monster brooch you could be in the morgue right now.'

That got Caitlin's attention. She agreed reluctantly to abandon the trip but was understandably worried about media intrusion. Helen tried to reassure her.

'We did not give out your name but I suspect someone at A&E in the hospital leaked it. They did not get your name right and at the moment some media seem to think it was Florence Scott Thomas who was stabbed, so she has been getting unwelcome attention on social media.'

'Poor Flo. It's the last thing she needs after all that shit she got about LGBT.'

Helen gave the writer some advice on handling the media when they inevitably discover who the victim really is. 'There are laws to prevent them naming or harassing victims but that won't stop some of them. Assuming of course you don't want to volunteer an interview to the Sun on 'the brooch that saved me' or 'my dog the hero'. Helen gave her a sly smile and the author laughed. 'Call us if they turn up here and we'll get rid of them. I'll give you my mobile and I'll ask for yours please – the one that doesn't go to voicemail – and I promise to keep you informed about anything we learn.'

The two policewomen stood to leave and the author suddenly seemed distraught. 'I didn't offer you coffee or anything. You must think me rude.'

'Don't mention it. After what you went through last night, you're the bloody heroine – not just Jasper.' This was Helen's gruff way of being sympathetic.

Having heard his name, Jasper began to bark, thinking no doubt of walkways.

* * *

Later that evening when Helen had gone off duty she popped into Rosie's flat where we had just finished eating. The two women had been friends since their schooldays in Currie outside Edinburgh and shared confidences. I had fallen foul of both at the conclusion of the Stolen Honours saga but had since been allowed back into their favour and more important to me, Rosie's affections.

'What's she like then?' was Rosie's first question to her friend. She too had read a few of Caitlin Mossiman's books.

'Really nice. Dead straight. And bloody lucky to be alive. That big brooch saved her life.'

'I know a GP in Glasgow who survived a similar attack by a psycho patient,' Rosie replied. 'Was this a psycho out on the prowl? God, less than a mile from here.'

'We just don't know. Could be a random or somebody who was obsessive about her. Florence Scott Thomas got all the media madness once again, but Caitlin Mossiman doesn't court controversy.'

'And we three were in both their company only a couple of nights ago,' I mused. I noticed the menu I had rescued on Rosie's mantelpiece and took it down. 'Did either of you look closely at the doodles on this menu?' I asked the two women, who shook their heads. 'Look at this. Against the names of the four celebrity crime writers there are little symbols.

Against Caitlin Mossiman's name there is a dagger. Is that a coincidence?'

'Synchronicity,' replied Rosie.

'What's that?' Helen asked, her educational level not matching that of the KC.

'Carl Jung coined it. Events that seem connected but have no causal link.'

'Why not just say coincidence?' Helen retorted.

I interrupted. 'The doodle against Florence Scott Thomas looks to me like a bomb. Am I crazy to suggest that if the symbols on the menu are connected, then she is in danger? I know one coincidence doesn't mean much but what if there is more to it than that.'

Helen Dyer couldn't resist another jibe. I sometimes wondered if she resented me having come into her best pal's life. 'Max, you have a wonderful imagination. Maybe you should ask one of your psychic chums to get out their crystal ball.'

I was stung into replying that it would not be the first death threat that the famous writer had received. Surely there would be no harm in checking it out? 'Besides it would give you a chance to meet her. She's apparently a very interesting lady.' Then I added provocatively, 'If she does get blown up and you didn't warn her, it might not look so good.'

DCI Dyer glared back, then suddenly changed her attitude. Whether it was to cover her back if the worst happened or the chance to meet the famous author which swayed her, I don't know, but she replied. 'I'll pop round see her. No harm in that. What are the other symbols? Let's have a look.'

We examined the menu card with a magnifying glass from Rosie's desk. Against the name of Anton Ross was a bottle with 'Poison' symbol written in it. Ronald MacKenzie had a gas mask.

Rosie asked,'Are these the doodles of someone who is bored by the speeches, or a fantasist who does not like the writers, or someone who knows what's going to happen?'

'I hope it's not anything sinister, otherwise we'll have a cull of crime writers on our hands. God, that would cause a sensation. Like worldwide.' Helen now seemed to be more willing to take my suggestion seriously. 'Who was sitting at that table anyway?'

Rosie answered as she looked down the list of guests and repeated what she had told me the other night, leaving out the negative comments on their characters. The forensic psychiatrist; the criminologist academic; the literary pundit; the police surgeon; and the lady GP from Liberton.

'None of them sound like nutters hiding in the bushes to stab the writer,' I said.

Helen Dyer endorsed my remark. 'Caitlin Mossiman described a young man wearing a balaclava so it doesn't look like there is any connection at all.

All these people are respected members of society anyway. Maybe it's just Max's vivid imagination working overtime,' she added, backtracking to her previous sceptical position.

Surprisingly it was Rosie who countered.

'Well, not all of them are 'respected'. By me anyway. You can forget the police surgeon and the GP. I know them both but the other three men are rumoured to be spiteful types and who's to know they didn't put Balaclava Man up to it.'

She did not know it at the time but that was exactly what had happened. But which of the three men, and what was their link to the failed assassin? Our seemingly fantastic speculations on the purpose of the doodles on the menu were to be surprisingly confirmed the very next day.

CHAPTER 4

Florence Scott Thomas herself opened the door of her home to DCI Helen Dyer. She knew they were coming after their telephone conversation earlier and had spotted the police car arrive via her home security system. DCI Dyer was accompanied this time by DS Mark Macormick, her 'bagman' who had expressed his eagerness to meet the famous crime writer. Her home was a large villa on the south side of Edinburgh. A three metre high wall surrounded the property, and the electrically operated entrance gates were fitted on either side with sentinels of security cameras. A curved lawn was flanked by rhododendron and azalea bushes, and the white walls of the villa were surrounded by colourful flower beds. The drive of yellow pea gravel forked around to the rear of the house toward a paved courtyard overlooked by a stable block around which security cameras nodded downwards. A red SUV with a recent numberplate was parked on the courtyard. The police car took the left fork, crunching over the gravel, and stopped in front of the entrance porch. The polished sky-blue front door opened as they arrived.

Dressed in baggy white linen trousers and a

yellow silk blouse, the willowy figure of the famous writer looked much thinner and prettier than her photographs in magazines. Her long blond hair was held back in a pony tail by a gold grip. Her makeup was discreet: flesh-colour lipstick and blue eye shadow accentuated her piercing blue eyes. Her mouth was slightly crooked, giving the impression of a quizzical expression.

'I was about to call you – or rather one of your colleagues – when you called me this morning. I expect it's about the intruder in the garden last night,' she began as they walked towards her. 'Sadly I've been forced to beef up my personal security in recent months and even employ a bodyguard. It was he who noticed the trespasser.' She stopped when they reached the steps and held out a hand. 'Flo Richards. Sorry, I'm gabbling. Do come in, I've asked for coffee in the conservatory.'

Her visitors noted she used her married name and not the one the public know her by. She led the way through a tiled hallway to a glass door and a large conservatory populated by pot-plants. In the centre was a large desk with laptop and to the side four chintz covered armchairs around a glass coffee table. An overhead fan gently stirred the air. They could have been in the Botanic Gardens but for the furniture. A home help brought in a tray with a cafetiére and chococlate biscuits.

'Mrs Richards, I should tell you right away that we are not here about your intruder.'

'Oh,' the author looked puzzled. 'Please call me Flo. So you didn't know about him? Well, I suppose if you're not from the same station that my security man called, you couldn't have known.'

'We actually did come to ask if you had noticed anything suspicious lately. We are from Gayfield Square police station. Our visit is in connection with the attack on your fellow writer Caitlin Mossiman. I expect you heard about it?'

'Heard about it? You bet! The sewer rats of social media were putting it about that it was me who was stabbed. How is Caitlin? I called her this morning after one of these people said it was actually her. She seemed OK but that could have been a front. You know we were both at a function only last Friday night. The Conan Doyle Hologram. Maybe I should start wearing costume jewellery like Caitlin. Saved her life apparently.'

The writer was gabbling again, as she had put it. The initial annoyance of being mistaken for the victim had given way to the nervy realisation that it might have been her. Having to employ personal security was a heavy price to pay for writing popular fiction and annoying the 'sewer rats'. Fortunately she could afford it.

Helen Dyer then explained that the attack on one

crime writer might be a precursor to an attack on another. The fact that they both had been in public at the same event might not be just be a coincidence. She made no reference to the menu doodles or to any of the other celebrity authors against whose names they had been drawn. 'But since we are here, Mrs.. er..Flo, perhaps we could look through the security camera footage and take a look around outside.'

'Sure, I can do that for you. Normally I would ask my security man to run you through the CCTV footage, but Sam is sleeping in his room upstairs. He stayed up all night after the camera beeped, to check the guy was not still lurking somewhere, and I insisted he got some sleep. My husband and I are going out tonight and he usually drives us, so I need him fresh for that.'

She led them to a basement cellar which was decked out with several security screens and the latest in surveillance equipment. She punched in the relevant time of the intrusion and we saw the shadowy figure of Balaclava Man steal across the paved courtyard carrying a sports bag and duck behind the red SUV.

'What's he doing?'

'Hiding from the cameras, I expect', replied the writer. He must have spotted them.'

'The cameras don't trigger floodlights?' DS Macormick queried.

'They used to but they were triggered so often by squirrels and birds that we took that feature out. It woke us up too often. The movement sensors are still there, and that's what picked him up.'

'How did he get into your garden? Presumably not through the electric gates.'

'No. The wall is pretty high and we put an electric fence on parts of it but there is a spot in the neighbour's garden where it would be easy to climb into ours. The neighbour's cat uses it to get into our garden by climbing onto a tree on their side and then jumps on the wall. I haven't the heart to electrocute the beast. Can you imagine the publicity that would get me? Cat killer?'

'Do you always leave your car out in the courtyard' the detective pursued.

'Not usually. We have a big double garage in the old stable block and two single ones for Sam's and Lichan's cars. Lichan (she pronounced it Lee-chan) is our other live-in employee. My husband always puts his car in the garage, but if I have a morning appointment I often leave my car out so that I can get away quickly and avoid all the manoeuvring.'

'And did you? Have a morning appointment?'

'Well, yes. But as I was preparing to leave, someone called to let me know the sewer rats had put my name online as the stabbing victim. I cancelled my hairdresser to avoid appearing in public and stayed at home. When it came out later that it was Caitlin who had been attacked, I called her on her private number. Originally I was thinking of taking my daughters Emily and Esmée to their school in Barnton before going to the hairdresser, but Nigel (that's my husband) volunteered instead to do it on his way to the Spire hospital where he had a clinic. So I did some writing until you showed up. I should explain that I like to take the girls to school when I can (despite the hellish morning traffic) but it's not often that I do. Lichan usually takes them in her car but she's gone to see her mother in England for a couple of days. I rely on her hugely, she's Taiwanese and she stays with us en famille. She babysits if we go out, cooks us all a Chinese meal once a week which is a highlight for the girls. She's also teaching them Chinese, and she has a black belt in Tae-kwon-do. So she doubles up as a bodyguard for the girls along with Sam.'

'She seems quite a girl. Has that proved necessary? To have a bodyguard for the girls.'

'Alas, yes. We used to live in another house in Edinburgh but it was less easy to feel secure there. We received a kidnap threat aimed at Emily and Esmée and that was when I employed Lichan in addition to Sam and we moved here. The very thought of the girls being taken makes my blood run cold. Your colleagues in the south side have been very good helping us set up a good security system and it's linked to them.'

'But they didn't attend last night?'

'No, because Sam called it in and explained he had searched the grounds and the guy had gone. We don't want to bother the police too often.'

Helen frowned when she thought of this family living under threat but apparently able to function normally, and be cheerful about it.

'Do you mind if we have a look round the garden and the courtyard?'

The DCI and her sergeant had the same thought and made straight for the courtyard where the author's car was still parked. Helen was wearing a skirt with her police uniform and so it was Mark who bent down in the spot where the camera had picked up Balaclava Man. He saw it immediately: a long metallic object clipped or magnetically stuck beneath the car on the driver's side. Neither of them had any experience of bombs but there was no doubt that was what it was.

While DCI Dyer went inside to break the news to the writer, DS Macormick called the Bomb Squad and prowled around the spot on the garden wall where the neighbour's cat apparently enjoyed trespassing. He could see no evident footprints but his forensic colleagues would soon be able to comb every inch for evidence.

Flo Richards was understandably shocked. Death threats she had had aplenty but actual attempts on her life, none. Other than the 'sewer rats' she had no enemies, was well-liked in her profession as a writer, and highly admired for the way she used her wealth as a benefactor of good causes. She admitted that there had been attempts at robbery of her home. She was in the Sunday Times rich list. Once when the couple were away in London the alarms had been triggered but the rapid intervention by the police meant no one had ever managed to get into their house. She had millions of fans around the world who loved her books, so why did someone want to kill her?

DCI Dyer invited the writer to suggest possible motives. Despite her world-class imagination she couldn't think of any, other than the hatemongers of the internet. Links to the attack on Caitlin Mossiman were not apparent. They knew each other as fellow writers – that was all.

Carefully Helen opened the topic of the dinner and the names at the table where the menu was found. There too she drew a blank. The writer said she knew none of them personally as was the case with most of the other people at the dinner except for Sir James Keillor who was a colleague and friend of her husband and from whom her invitation had come.

The annoying realisation that Max Quillan had

been right once again was quickly put to the back of her mind as she tried to alleviate the trauma she thought the famous writer must be experiencing. The gruff DCI was not a natural counsellor, but she tried her best by suggesting to Mrs Richards that she should concentrate on the fact that she had escaped death, as had her daughters. The writer did not seem to need her clumsy but well-meant reassurances, nodding simply in response. After all, telling her she had escaped from an attacker who was still out there was hardly reassuring. Florence Scott Thomas was made of sterner stuff than her slight physique might have suggested. She indicated to the detective that she needed privacy to make some calls which came as a relief to Helen Dyer. As a matter of urgency she now needed to track down the other two writers whose names had been marked on the menu.

CHAPTER 5

The journey to Longforgan took an hour, on dual carriageway all the way. From Edinburgh we crossed the Forth Bridge, then went north up the M90 and after crossing the Tay at Friarton Bridge, drove east along the flat landscape of the Carse of Gowrie. Castle Huntly is on the south side of the village and its tower was easily seen as we approached. The formalities to be endured to visit Rosie's son Tom were not as restrictive as I had imagined. HMP Castle Huntly is an 'open prison' and we were expected.

Tom Sanderson, the name in which his birth was registered by his adoptive parents, had grown up in Greenock but after numerous incidents of scams, lies and eventually a prison sentence for fraud, his adoptive parents had severed relations when he was aged twenty. Rosie told me during our drive that his adoptive father now had lung cancer and his wife was in poor health. She had contacted them after Tom had surfaced in her life. They apparently had given Tom a loving home and she had nothing but sympathy and admiration for them. Coping with serious illness and a wayward son at the same time had proved too much for them. They had disinherited him and were spending what savings they had on trying to make their own last years as comfortable as possible.

'I guess Tom thought I might be a softer touch when his parents closed the door on any future finance,' Rosie confided with more than a trace of bitterness. I could tell that she was steeling herself for any scams that might come her way from a conman son. 'I want your opinion on Tom,' she said as we waited to enter the prison. 'He's charming and you will most likely take to him at first but beware. It's the end game that worries me.'

Rosie was usually more generous in her appraisal of people, even the criminals she defended in court. But here was her Achilles heel, a son who was capable of taking savings from elderly vulnerable people and seemingly feeling no guilt.

We were shown into a large lounge and sat on a settee waiting. Tom entered from a door at the other side of the room and we stood to greet him. He was a tall, clean-shaven man in his twenties. His dark curly hair had been allowed to grow, which gave him a boyish appearance. His eyes were definitely his mother's but wore a sad expression. After embracing Rosie, to my surprise he greeted me with enthusiasm.

'Max, I've been dying to meet you. Rosie told me something about meeting you at the Arthur Conan Doyle Centre and then how you worked out where the guys who stole the Crown Jewels were hiding them. Brilliant!'

'Well, with a little help from my friends, or rather Rosie's friend Helen.'

'Ah,' he laughed, 'The formidable DCI Dyer. The Dobermann of the Edinburgh 'polis'.' His accent showed his west coast upbringing.

We spent the next half hour discussing the arrangements for his release at the end of the month. Rosie, in dealing with her clients, was familiar with all the rules and regulations about probation and parole (I was not sure which was which and she tried to explain). Tom would be receiving income support plus a room in a hostel in Edinburgh (thank God for that, I selfishly thought, considering my frequent visits to her Eglinton Crescent flat). Rosie had promised to help with the rent and finding him work. In order to save Rosie giving up a work day to collect him on his release, I found myself talked by Tom into driving up to Longforgan. I did not dare look at Rosie's expression as it meant borrowing her car. I had no car of my own and did not need one.

'It will give us a chance to get to know each other,' he continued, 'But enough of me, what have you two been up to? I gather you were at that event where Conan Doyle appeared as a hologram. Cool! And Rosie said last time she was here that you were going to the dinner with famous crime writers, how was that? Who was all there?'

We told him the dinner was just a front for the speeches which he would soon be able to see in a documentary, and that the guests had been chosen to represent different facets of the great man's life. Rosie brought out a photocopy of the menu I had rescued (the original now being with Helen's forensics people).

'It's a pretty eclectic lot but then old Arthur had a huge number of interests. Don't suppose you will know any of the people. They're all from Edinburgh,' said Rosie as she handed him the list which he scrutinised.

'Oh, but I do. Apart from you two and Dobermann Dyer there are three people I have seen here at Castle Huntly, visiting.' He pointed with his finger at the names of three people who had sat at the table under which I had found the menu.

'Who were they visiting?' I asked him.

'A very nasty piece of work who committed rape and murder while he was a juvenile. William 'Billy' McDade. He was found to be insane and sent to Carstairs where he met this guy.' He pointed at the name of Sir Martin Forbes-Graham. He was the forensic psychiatrist at his trial and he went on to treat him at Carstairs where he is a visiting consultant. According to the shrink, Billy boy made great progress under his care, and was sent here for assessment and possible release back into the community. He got it last month.'

Rosie let out a sound expressing disgust and I asked if the other two had visited the same man.

'Yep. The shrink came several times but these two came only once each. I think Billy boy gave them the bum's rush.'

'In what way?'

'Well, I should tell you first that McDade became a bit of celebrity after he got out of Carstairs. As he was a juvenile he couldn't be named in the media at the time of his trial, but when he was in Carstairs they put him in a Special Unit for people with an artistic talent and his talent was sculptures in wood. They sold for thousands. So when he got his transfer here thanks to Sir Martin the Shrink, it all came out and made him famous. Some people said he should never get out because of his crimes but the arty mob got on his case and said he had (I'm quoting here) 'redeemed himself through his talents', although I'm damned if I see how chiselling a block of wood makes up for chiselling people and raping underage girls.'

I couldn't have put it better myself. I was beginning to like Tom.

Rosie intervened to bring Tom back to the visits by the other two men. 'You said they only came once each. Why was that?'

'He had become a celebrity. The Jimmy Boyle

of Castle Huntly. Bad boy made good through art. Lots of people wanted to come and do features on him, interview him but the authorities didn't allow it. Said it would affect his rehabilitation but those two wrote to him and made a pitch. He requested them as visitors and they came. I think he wanted to humiliate them. I said he gave them the bums rush, but I think it was mutual. They found out what he was really like.'

'What was he like?' I interrupted. 'Did you get to know him?'

'Not really. Truth is I steered well clear of him. He was a psychopathic bastard who got off on cruelty. Do you remember a sci-fi film from the fifties called the Midwich Cuckoos? It was about a UFO which was full of blond emotionless zombies who tried to take over the world. Billy looks like one of them, blond, handsome and totally without feelings or personality. Some of his fans and supporters projected their idea of what they thought he was like inside onto this blank screen, and saw what they wanted. I would never have joked with him or called him the Carstairs Cuckoo (I didn't want a chisel in my head) but I did get him talking once, that's how I know about what these other two men wanted. He was boasting about it afterwards, laughing at how much he despised them.'

'What did they want with him?'

'A bit of his fame perhaps, but in different ways. One of them was a so-called Criminologist, a mincing queer who I think fancied him. He said he wanted to do an academic study on Billy's upbringing in Dundee and how it had influenced him to commit his crimes. Bullshit if you ask me and Billy didn't buy it either. Told him to get lost. He spotted the way the guy looked at him. He's a pretty boy and after he went to prison he soon learned how to fend off unwanted attention.'

Probably with a chisel, I thought. 'And the other one? The literary guy, Adrian Frei. What did he want?'

'Something similar. He wanted to write a book with or about Billy McDade telling the story of his life. It wasn't going to be a ghost autobiography. Frei wanted his name on the cover. Billy told him he was going to let his sculptures do the talking not words which someone else wrote. End of story.'

Our visit to Tom gave us unexpected information linking the names on the menu to a known criminal. Rosie had a consultation with a client, so we took our leave of Tom and hastened back to Edinburgh. What Tom had told us would be of interest to DCI Dyer. I smiled at Tom's nickname for her. Not wholly inappropriate in my opinion.

As soon as we got in the car, Rosie asked my opinion on Tom. I had no difficulty in being positive.

'He seems sincere to me. He was very open with us and I hope when he gets out his prospects will improve. I liked him a lot. Soon you will have two men in your life and both of them unemployed.'

'I know,' she grunted and began to exceed the speed limit until I gently pointed out we were doing 90 mph. Thankfully we were not in sight of any speed cameras. It was not until we were over the Forth Bridge that we talked about the discovery that three of the men at the marked menu table had links with a convicted killer recently released from prison. We had not yet learned what Helen Dyer had uncovered under Florence Scott Thomas's car and which had sent her swiftly to the homes of the other celebrity crime writers.

Chapter 6

Anton Ross lived in the area of Edinburgh known as Colinton. Wedged between Colinton Village and Baberton are several large houses with their own gardens. Some have been divided but Anton Ross and his wife had the whole house. No security cameras or electric sensors on the walls were apparent but the author did not seem to attract any hostility. His beginnings in the mining village and the rebellious character of the detective he created, had made him a man of the people. His easy generous manner towards other writers when being interviewed had earned him much popularity in the publishing world as had his charity work. His fictional detective was based on a retired policeman who frequented a real city centre pub which was now featured by tourist guides in their walking tours. But not many people knew the author lived in Edinburgh or was a rich as he was.

Fortunately Anton Ross was at home when DCI Dyer called ahead to arrange a visit. She and DS Macormick were both still in uniform when they rang the bell as they had come straight from the Richard's home. The famous author was in a track suit and had either been out jogging or exercising in his own gym as his face was lathered in sweat. 'Forgive the sweaty appearance, please, officers. I just had time to make my daily ten miles target before you arrived. Do come in.'

'Running or on a bike?' asked the detective sergeant.

'A bike, but it stands still in my house while I pedal,' the writer laughed. He was clearly a man of good humour.

When they asked him if he has had any intruders or had any death threats recently, he said he had neither but surprised them by guessing why they were there. 'Caitlin is a friend of mine and I gather she was the victim of the attempted stabbing the night before last. We were both at a function last week – the Conan Doyle event – and I suppose you need to check on whether there is any link.'

'That's very astute of you, Mr Ross,' said DS Macormick. 'It is the reason we are here but the attack on Ms Mossiman has already been followed by a very serious attempt on the life of someone else.' He looked at DCI Dyer for confirmation that he could share the information about the bomb at Florence Scott Thomas's home. She nodded as there was no way they could keep this quiet any longer. 'I'm afraid there has been a bomb placed under the car of another writer who was at the dinner.'

'Not Flo?' He looked genuinely shocked. 'Is she

OK?'

Helen entered the conversation. 'Yes, she's fine. A bit shaken but thankfully she had not taken her car out this morning and when we called at her home and looked underneath the car, there it was. The Bomb Squad are there now so we will know in the next hour whether it is a fake or the real thing. Obviously we can't take any chances. The attack on Ms Caitlin Mossiman was no fake. She was saved because the knife bounced off her brooch. Why did you assume it was Florence Scott Thomas and not the other writer?'

'Because Ronnie does not attract the same venom that Flo does, and maybe it was a matter of time before one of these internet trolls made good on their threats.'

'Yes, both victims were at the same dinner less than a week ago. And so were you and Ronald MacKenzie. So we wanted to make sure you and he were not intended targets also.' She had no intention of saying anything about the marked menu to anyone outside her own team.

'That's very good of you,' said the writer. 'Always assuming we had nothing to do with it,' he added laughingly, until he looked at their faces and realised the seriousness of the situation. 'I'm sorry, it just seems too ludicrous for words. It's like a plot in one of my books – or the books that any one of the four of us might have written. 'The Crimewriter Killer'. Not a bad title.' He was beginning to regain his good humour. 'Maybe you should pull in Val McDermid for questioning, ask her if she is trying to get rid of the opposition!' He beamed. 'Don't be shocked, officers, I'm actually a great friend of Val and it's just the kind of plot she would love. In fiction of course.' He subsided back into his armchair, shaking his head and muttering 'Unbelievable'.

'I know you, like us, are relieved that nothing came of these attacks. As yet we have no suspects, no reason why these attacks could have taken place but it's too coincidental that they link to a recent event. It could be that the female writers were chosen as easier targets but we have to ask you again if there have been any events, communications or actions since that dinner which have been out of the ordinary? We'll be asking Mr MacKenzie the same thing.'

'I've had nothing by way of my security cameras. They may not have been visible as you came in but that's the point – I want them to remain discreetly out of sight in the trees. As for communications I get a lot of reader feedback via my publisher and publicist but nothing sinister of late. A few years ago I had dealings with a nutter in the USA, if that's not a tautology, who claimed that I had plagiarised his work and he wanted millions of dollars in a lawsuit. I told him I was flattered to be compared to him and never heard from him again. Nothing too nasty by way of reviews by critics either. There was one review last year in the Sunday Times by one of the people at that Conan Doyle dinner - Adrian Frei. That was a bit venomous but most people know he is a frustrated crime writer who can't get published. He occasionally writes pieces disparaging crime writing as literary porn on the same low level as sci-fi but he's harmless. He promised to give the Conan Doyle thing a big puff and the irritating thing is that people read him. Can't see him creeping around Queen Street Gardens at night, though. Mind you I could see Jason Dunnet but it wouldn't be women he was after. I hope you're not writing this down, are you? I shall deny I said it.'

'Don't worry, sir. We won't tell, as long as you don't write us up in your next book as stumbling plods.'

'Can't do that, Sergeant. Especially as it looks as if you saved her life by looking under her car and finding that bomb. Well done.'

Helen smiled gratefully. 'You mentioned Jason Dunnet who was at the dinner. Why was he there?'

'A very good question, DCI Dyer. He is known to have a toxic hatred of crime writing. Claims we don't have the first idea of the criminal mind and instead of inventing serial killers everywhere we should look at the social and political conditions that lead to people committing crimes. All very grim. He should lighten up and realise that the books we write are a form of entertainment, not social analysis. By the way, I don't know why he came to the dinner but I know how. He stole the invitation that went to the University department in which he works. Sir James told me at the dinner that the bugger virtually dared them to take it away from him. I didn't recognise you at first in your uniform, but I know you got your invitation owing to the influence of your friend the lovely Rosamunde. He told me that as well.'

Helen was annoyed by how much the author seemed to know about her dinner invitation so she returned to the subject of other more relevant things he might have noticed. 'Think carefully, sir, have you had any visitors, callers or calls in the past few days which might in retrospect seem suspicious?'

'Well a delivery guy came to the door yesterday. My wife was here and signed for the parcel. He was perfectly legit and left me a presentation box with a bottle of an expensive malt, my favourite tipple, aged 16 years. Now that is unusual, eh? It came with a note from a Scots Canadian who said he enjoyed my books and he knew I would not drink too much of it, unlike Madsen. That's my detective in case neither of you read my stuff.'

'Can we see the bottle, sir? And the card that came with it, please.'

Ross went to a drinks cupboard and brought out a box containing a bottle of Macallan. Macormick swiftly put on a pair of plastic gloves and drew the bottle out of the box. He sniffed around the cap and gently turned the seal around the top, which moved, suggesting it had been taken off then replaced. He looked meaningfully at his senior colleague.

'I'm sorry but we need to take this away, Mr Ross,' said DCI Dyer. We will need a small sample but I promise you, we will not drink it. Can we have the note which came with it, please.'

DS Macormick took the card, opened it still wearing his protective gloves, and read aloud. 'To the best detective writer in the world from a Scots Canadian. You won't drink it all at once as Madsen might have done.' He raised his eyebrows and turned to the writer. 'Not signed. The tip-off which led us here suggested that you might have been sent something with poison in it. If this whisky bottle was tampered with then you wouldn't have drunk all of it anyway. You might not have been alive to do so.'

The cheerful face of the celebrity author had assumed a pale expression and the sweat on his brow was not now from his exercise bicycle. He went in search of his wife to tell her the grim news and the detectives took away the suspect bottle. There would have to be overtime at the Forensics Lab.

Urgent attempts to track down Ronald

MacKenzie had eventually succeeded in locating him in London at his publishers. He and his wife had stayed the previous night at his club. He was accorded a direct call from the Assistant Chief Constable whom he knew socially (their sons had been at the same school). When the level of the threat was explained to him he promised to take the train north in the morning. Apparently he was to be the main speaker at a posh dinner that evening and reluctant to cancel. He promised to say nothing to anyone including his publisher and gave permission for the police to pick up keys to his home from a neighbour.

CHAPTER 7

Having dropped the bottle of whisky at the lab, and DS Macormick at the station, DCI Dyer continued across Edinburgh to Ronald MacKenzie's home on Leith Links where two other members of her team were waiting outside. DI Roderick Cairns and DC Natalie Barnes were with an employee of British Gas (or was it Scottish Gas? - they seemed to use the terms interchangeably to the confusion of customers). They already had the keys to MacKenzie's home.

'Right,' said DCI Dyer, 'Let's do this. I want a thorough check of all the gas inlets and appliances in the house. Then we search it for gas cylinders of any kind. Even camping gas. Look in the bathroom to see if someone could have tampered with an aerosol.' She had no idea how they could check an aerosol spray but she was now fired up and well aware the case had assumed huge importance.

'Excuse me, Ma'm,' the bright DC Barnes put in. She was regarded by the DCI as 'a bit of a flake' after she had been off ill twice with Covid, but her work was excellent. 'If we couldn't get in until we had the keys, perhaps the person who targeted these other people would have been stymied as well and tried something outside. Maybe the gas main.' The DCI looked at her stonily, but realised the girl was right.

'Yes, we should start with the exterior, then we go in and search everywhere. Let's go.'

It was not long before they found what they were looking for. A gas cylinder labelled hydrogen was lying on its side against the rear of the house and a tube went from the cylinder through a hole which had been made in the glass of a barred window in a downstairs room. The gas cylinder valve had been opened slightly and a colourless odourless gas was entering the room and mixing with the air inside. Once a certain level of hydrogen/oxygen had been reached, any spark or flame would cause an explosion of considerable intensity. The room chosen for the gas to enter was next to the kitchen where a gas hob was visible to them as they stood looking into the house. When someone turned it on this would have triggered an explosion, always assuming a spark from something else had not got there first.

Helen Dyer turned to DC Barnes. 'Nat, I owe you a large drink. I reckon you saved us all from walking into an inferno.' She turned to the Gas Board man. 'We clearly have a gas leak here and it's bloody dangerous. What do you want us to do?'

The man looked apprehensive. 'We'll have to get out of here. Pronto. I take it you turned off the valve on the cylinder? Well, I'll have to take the keys and wait for the team to open the house and find how much gas is in there, open all the windows and doors and air it completely. You'll need to close the road in case there's an electric timer set somewhere to spark it into action. I'm guessing you folks are here because there's a crime element to all this. In fact I'm sure your Bomb Squad people will need to take a look before we go in. I take there is no one inside, that's why you had to get the keys?'

'Yes, the owners are in London. Lucky them. OK, we'll call the Bomb boys and close the road, and leave you to follow your usual gas leak protocols.' She sighed. This had turned into a bigger case than she would have liked to handle and there was still no link between Balaclava man and the marked menu card. She knew she had better go straight to the top floor of Police Scotland HQ and report the latest development.

The Assistant Chief Constable who had spoken to Ronald MacKenzie was stunned when he heard that the police now had four attempted murders on their hands, all of famous people. He knew that would bring huge media attention. Helen Dyer was afraid she was about to lose the case, and perhaps part of her actually wanted that to happen. She was shown into ACC Simon Barton's office at Police Scotland's Fettes Avenue HQ and briefed him on what had happened since the attack on Caitlin Mossiman. He wanted to know more about the link to the Conan Doyle dinner and she showed him the marked menu.

'I agree with you, it's beyond coincidence that these symbols against the names of the actual attempted murder victims are not connected in some way. How did you get this menu?'

'It was picked up under one of the tables by Max Quillan after the dinner. He was a guest at the dinner as was I, sir.'

'Not him again. The one who tipped us off where to find the Crown Jewels. Does he go looking for crime waves to surf?'

'He's actually the partner of a good friend of mine, Rosamunde Michelle KC. I think you know her, sir.'

'Indeed I do. But tell me more about this dinner table of suspects and who was at it. They are obviously not those who stabbed Caitlin Mossiman or were caught on the camera at Florence Scott Thomas's home.'

'No, sir. The assailant was a young, athletic person, and none at that table are either of those things. The only motive that has been suggested is that three of the people at the table dislike crime writers. One of them might have hired Balaclava Man to attack the famous authors.'

'Well he made an arse of it didn't he? Ran off when the dog bit him, planted a bomb which you discovered. Well we assume the Bomb Squad will tell us it was a bomb. Then you spotted his poisoned whisky before Anton Ross drank it (again I'm assuming the lab will confirm that). Finally you trumped him again down at Ronnie's house in Leith Links. Congratulations.'

Helen Dyer was delighted he had said 'you' and not 'we' but was not prepared for what came next. She carried on, 'Unfortunately we still don't have a lead on him. It's only day two and I was about to start talking to those at that table, but in view of the fame of the victims, I wanted to be sure of my ground. Once the four attacks become public, it will start a media storm.'

'I think you need help with this, Helen, and that's why I have to take you off as SIO on the case. You've done really well in heading off...well, three attempted murders. That means a lot. But as you said yourself, you and your pal Rosamunde were both at this dinner and we can't ignore the fact the attacks are linked to the dinner menu. And of course our friend Quillan was there too. When we get this killer we may have challenges from the defence because you were personally at the dinner.'

The change from 'you' to 'we' had not gone unnoticed by Helen and she could hardly argue but it hurt to have to take a back seat when she had enjoyed such success so far.

'What about my team, sir? We have tried to keep this quiet and the less people know about the menu connection the better. Can they stay on the case?'

'Yes, of course. Although these writers are all famous people, the culprit is obviously someone with local knowledge. So I need your team since if I bring someone from Scotland Yard they would be lost in our city. Your team are already familiar with the case and they know Edinburgh. I'm going to ask DCS David Durrant from Glasgow to come through and take over. You will still be involved and will assist but not as the SIO. Don't take this as a demotion. In fact I'm going to put you down for a recommendation for preventing these attacks. Tell it to your team that way. First off I want an officer at the home of each of these writers overnight until we make an arrest. Someone will also have to meet Ronnie MacKenzie and his wife off the London train tomorrow and take him to his house. Presumably the BS team and the Gas Board will have it cleared by later today. Did your lad Macormick take the cylinder away for fingerprints?'

'Not yet, sir. But I'll see it's done and if you can authorise the extra officers to stay at the home of the writers, I'll get them briefed.' She felt a curious mixture of relief that the weight of responsibility had been lifted while at the same time regret she was not in charge any more. 'One more thing, sir. You mentioned Max Quillan. He and I have a love-hate relationship but he was the one who made the connection with the marked menu. Do I have permission at least to tell him he was right about the perceived threat to the crime writers?'

'Yes, but tell him he has to keep it totally confidential. And that goes for that KC pal of yours.'

As she was briefing her team the next morning about the change of Senior Investigating Officer to DCS Durrant, a call came in from the Bomb Squad. The device under Florence Scott Thomas's car was a crude bomb using nitroglycerine. The glycerine and nitric acid were in separate parts of the device and when the car got on the road the movement of the vehicle would cause the chemicals to mix. At ordinary temperatures the mixture was unstable and would explode.

The results on the whisky bottle were also back. Once the seal around the top was loosened and had slid off the neck, the cork stopper was easy to remove (and put back afterwards). Cyanide had been introduced into the whisky in sufficient quantity to kill anyone who drank it. Both methods were simple, one might even say amateurish, but they could easily have worked had they not been headed off by the police. The same was true of the hydrogen cylinder device.

Helen tried to spread a little of the credit she had been given by the ACC among her team but she knew that the largest portion should go to Max Quillan. She owed it to him to explain how his idea had saved the lives of three of the four writers. It was mid evening when she arrived at Rosie's flat where she and Max were waiting.

* * *

I (Max) am taking over the story as I am involved in the next part of it.

'Have you eaten?' Rosie asked her friend whose diet did her chunky physique no favours. 'You can't go on keeping these silly hours and skipping proper meals. We've kept you some kedgeree and here's a glass of Chablis to wash it down.'

The DCI sat at the table and started to speak. Rosie stopped her and told her to eat while she explained what we had learned from Tom at Castle Huntly.

When Helen finished eating, she dropped her bombshell. 'I'm off the case.'

'What!' we both exclaimed. 'How can they do that?'

She then recounted her interview with ACC Barton and how he had lauded her and then sidelined her. 'That's not the most important thing that happened today. What I am about to tell you is in strict confidence and only because you, Max, are owed huge thanks not simply by me but by three crime writers who might not be alive had you not pushed me to go and visit them about the marks on the menu.'

I was stunned into silence.

She continued. 'There was a bomb under Mrs Richards' car. It didn't go off 'cos she didn't use it and instead phoned Caitlin Mossiman to offer support. Then the doodle of the 'poison' bottle turned out to be real as well. Anton Ross got a bottle of expensive malt delivered from a 'fan' but it was laced with cyanide, and we intercepted it in time. Finally, Ronald MacKenzie had gone to London yesterday but someone deposited a cylinder of hydrogen gas which was leaking into his house and would have ignited had he or his wife used the gas ring in the kitchen. Four attempted murders and all of them failed more by good fortune than anything.'

'They were all very amateurish in one way,' I said. 'No plastic explosive or guns or anything like professional criminals might use. Yet they all show huge planning, knowledge of the targets and their homes. The materials used were all assembled in advance (perhaps not the knife in the gardens attack) and the attacks were more or less timed to take place in a twenty four hour window.'

'By the same person,' Rosie added. 'Whom we still believe must be linked to someone at that dinner. One of the three at that table. All of whom visited Billy McDade at Castle Huntly. What do you think, Helen? Is William 'Billy the kid' McDade our killer?'

'I must say it looks like it. As I told you, it's not my case any more but I will think of a way to get this info to DCS Durrant and the team. They already have the menu link so I imagine they will start to interview the three men who visited McDade at Longforgan. If he turns out to be the killer and we have forensic evidence to convict him, we need to know who asked him to do it and why.'

'Whoever planned all this is devious and clever,' I added. 'I'm certain they will have gone to a considerable length to avoid being linked to McDade. It's almost like they are playing a game, using McDade as a proxy. He must have met his evil mentor somewhere sometime and he must have been given the tools to finish the job. I mean, you don't get those chemicals over the counter. There must be a trail there which will lead to the right guy. I nearly said 'lead us' but none of us are now involved.'

'Well, I still am,' replied Helen. 'In a manner of speaking. I can whisper in the right ears but I can't be seen talking to any suspects.'

'I can,' I said. 'Your ACC may not like it but he can't stop me talking to the forensic shrink, the criminologist and the literary guy to ask them if they are willing to give a Tuesday Talk at the Arthur Conan Doyle Centre. I will ask them in a way they will politely decline (or maybe not so politely after I ask them what they know about Billy McDade). Of course I won't go near McDade himself but I have an idea of how we can perhaps get him to talk. I will need Rosie's permission though.'

'And in what way do you need my permission for that?' asked Rosie.

'The only person known to us with a connection to McDade is your son Tom. They may not have been pals at Castle Huntly but when Tom gets out soon and arrives in Edinburgh he could contact McDade and try to find out something, ask for his advice about life after prison.'

'And get a hatchet in his head for asking?'

'If necessary I will go along and shadow the meeting. McDade doesn't know what I look like.'

Rosie looked far from convinced.

Helen looked worried. 'Max, be very careful. This guy is a psycho, never mind what strings Forbes-Graham pulled to get him out of Carstairs. He has killed before and he would have killed Caitlin Mossiman but for that blessed brooch. And he has some powerful patrons for his sculpture work.'

I promised I would be careful and would tell her anything I might get from the three meetings. In fact I would record them secretly on my phone, I said. But I would need to find out where McDade was living and what he was doing in Edinburgh if Helen could help me. Unless of course the police arrest him before Tom and I could get to him.

CHAPTER 8

Rosie already had a mobile number for Sir Martin Forbes-Graham from the time he had invited her out to dinner. So I began with him, trotting out my story about wanting to find new speakers for Tuesday Talks. To my surprise, he countered by inviting me to the New Club for lunch, the establishment club in mid Princes Street.

'I'm sure you would have taken me to somewhere delightful but as you probably know, my wife is in the House of Lords and so I spend a lot of time in London. I get into the New Club so little these days that my subscription needs to be used to make it worthwhile.'

I agreed readily and went to the address in Princes Street but searched in vain for the entrance until I saw a nondescript door between two store fronts, one of which was Ann Summers lingerie. The door disguises the Tardis that lurks on the upper floors where the prominenti of Edinburgh can mix with their own professions and classes. I was buzzed in and when I emerged from the elevator on the first floor opposite the reception, Forbes-Graham was waiting for me in the large vestibule wearing a pin striped suit and light blue silk tie, his silver hair brushed back from his temples. Looking every bit like Christopher Plummer.

'So you're the lovely Rosamunde's latest squeeze?' he began, and held out a limp hand. 'Pleased to meet you.' It seemed designed to put me down. The setting, the reference to Rosie, and the deliberate avoidance of the fact we had both been guests at the Conan Doyle dinner. Maybe he had been too busy doodling on his menu to have seen my name on the guest list.

We skipped an aperitif. He said he had to go to Carstairs in the afternoon to see a patient. Having chosen the venue and time for our meeting, it was yet another little put-down, a way of saying he was too busy to linger over lunch with the likes of me. We both chose the same main course, a venison stew with roast potatoes, and while we waited for it and sipped at the Club claret, I began my spiel about the Tuesday Talks. He smiled, no, that would not do justice to the smug expression on his face as he shook his head before I had finished my first sentence.

'No, Max, I'm afraid the answer is no. I don't have a scintilla of credence in the paranormal or whatever you want to call it. Conan Doyle was a fool, duped into believing all that stuff. If you want to be kind you might say he was compensating for the death of his son in the Great War when he converted to spiritualism.'

Sir Martin was clearly not a person who wanted to be kind. I was tempted to argue that ACD's interest pre-dated the death of his son but I was there to draw him out, not disagree with him.

'We do have sceptical speakers from time to time,' I feebly offered. 'Do you not meet in the course of your psychiatric work people who believe they are talking to the dead? Perhaps you even have an explanation for it.'

'Certainly I do. It is most probably due to a lesion in the pre-frontal cortex or full blown schizophrenia. I must tell you, however, that I am an atheist of the deepest hue, a disciple of Dawkins if he would have me. We are animals: we breed, enjoy our habitat and then we die. End of story. But I also value my reputation as a physician. To be advertised as speaking to the kind of people who fete so-called mediums in your building will hardly enhance it. Present company excepted of course.' Again the smug smile.

'I'm tempted,' I countered, 'to offer my apologies for wasting your time and eating this lunch on false pretences.'

He waved his hand dismissively. 'As I told you, I need to lunch here to justify my subscription. You seemed an interesting prospect.' Each little dart was chosen to deflate his opponent.

I decided to go on the front foot. 'But you

accepted, or obtained, an invitation to the Conan Doyle dinner despite your low opinion of the man?'

'I went there to observe the writers who were speaking. They make a fortune out of writing about the criminal mind and yet they do not understand it. I found it amusing that everyone wants to canonise old Sir Arthur. His religion is a rehashed form of Manichaeanism, seeing the world as a battle of good and evil, matter and spirit. These writers spin their yarns about good versus evil in a similar dualistic way.'

'The Cathars I teach about in my courses believed the same thing.'

'There is no spirit, no good as such, no evil. It is all material, animal.'

We had finished our main course and were waiting for our summer pudding, so Sir Martin decided to continue his diatribe. 'People invent stories they want to believe in. Take this one for instance: We hold these truths to be self-evident, that all men are created equal, that they are endowed by their Creator with certain unalienable Rights, that among these are Life, Liberty and the pursuit of Happiness. What a lot of tosh. We are not equal in the slightest. Never will be or should be redefined as equals. As for 'rights' - that is a dream contradicted by the reality we see around us in the world where dog eats dog, and pursues what his genes tell him to do. No rights about it.'

'What does your wife think of your views? She's a Human Rights lawyer isn't she.' He seemed to be pleased at my provocation, his opponent was showing some fight.

'I could say, don't bring my wife into this, but I won't. We have opposite views of the world and so we don't discuss them. We argue about harmless topics like politics and art. You should hear us debating opera performances. Worse than PMQs in the Commons.'

I was delighted to have drawn him out about his beliefs, but now was the time to play my ace. 'I was recently up at Castle Huntly near Longforgan and your name came up. I gather you visit a former patient there...'

His head was already moving from side to side. 'I don't discuss former patients. Have you not heard of doctor patient confidentiality?' His face coloured.

I had evidently stung and surprised him by making the link to McDade.

'Can we not even discuss his art, his talent as a sculptor?'

'Perhaps. He's very talented. But he is now paroled and he is no longer my patient. I don't know where he stays, I gather he is now working in the Woodpecker Project. I gave them a reference.'

That last disclosure was interesting. I did not

believe him for a minute that he was not aware where McDade stayed. 'Why would Jason Dunnet and Adrian Frei have visited him at Longforgan?' I pursued, determined to use this opportunity before he clammed up.

'I have no idea. You must ask them yourself. Now if you have finished your lunch, I must be going as I need to get to Carstairs.'

I thanked him for lunch, glad I had seen him close up, unpleasant as it had been. But was he responsible for targeting the crime writers? Before I could decide that I still had two other candidates to quiz about the symbols on the menu.

There is only so much a person can bear sitting opposite unpleasant people at a meal, so my next appointment was with Jason Dunnet in a pub on the South side where I could take my leave easily. It was near to his room in the Criminology Department and by coincidence it happened to be the one in which Anton Ross's fictional detective was a regular.

He was already standing tall at the bar at 5pm when I entered, holding court to a couple of young male students, with a pint in his hand. He was like a younger version of Stephen Fry and had the habit of sweeping back a quiff of dark hair from his temple. When I introduced myself as the person who had telephoned him, recognition dawned.

'You were at the Conan Doyle dinner!

Representing some centre or other. Ah, that is the one you want me to come and talk at on a Tuesday. Come and let's get a table so that I can tell you why I don't want to do it.'

Good, I thought. I can get straight to the real reason I came to see him. I followed him to a seat in the depths of the bar.

'I appreciate your time,' I began.

'And I will appreciate yours even more if you can buy me a refill when I have finished this,' he replied, swallowing the dregs of his beer glass. I dutifully went to the bar and returned to the table with two pints of the draught beer he had specified.

'I suspected you might turn me down,' I admitted. 'But there is another subject I wanted to raise with you.'

His eyebrows shot up. 'Indeed?' He managed to make even one word sound a little camp and suggestive. 'I hope you don't want my views on so-called crime writers. I would have to use some bad words. I try to ration myself to one lecture a year in which I describe their crimes against writing and against my friends the criminals. But I can hear your ratiocination gears grinding. You were at that dinner and you wonder how on earth I was there with views like mine. Well, I'd better tell you. I was naughty. The invite came to the department and I asked the Dean if I could go. He is from another department and he hadn't heard of my allergy to crime writing so I went. Principally it was a visit to the zoo to see how the animals behaved. I thought it all rather amusing.'

'Did you keep your menu?' I asked.

'Oh yes, I'm going to have it framed. All those crime writers guests listed and there in the midst is little me, Daniel among the lions of low literature.'

'Actually, I have something else I wanted to ask you. Last week I was visiting someone at HMP Castle Huntly and your name came up, as having visited Billy McDade...'

The eyebrows shot up again.'My goodness you do get about. Yes, I was there visiting beautiful Billy. Once and once only. I had a proposition for him. Not the kind you might imagine. I wanted to do a serious study with him going through his life story, the influences on him, family life (or rather lack of it), his period with drugs. He would have made an excellent academic case study. You see I may be a bit of showman but I am a serious psychologist as well as a criminologist. I also one of those Behaviourist beasts who follow B.F. Skinner and all that. To give you the shorthand version. Criminals are made by their environment, their upbringing, their parents' fuck-ups. They are virtually programmed to be what they become and Billy is a classic case. He would have been ideal but he turned me down flat. Looked at me with those ice-cool blue eyes and just walked away. I was actually hurt because I thought I was doing the boy a favour. From what I hear though, he's doing well for himself as a sculptor. He's working here in Edinburgh in some community project. Good luck to him.'

'You've not tried to persuade him again?'

'No – and I won't. The more I thought about it the more I realise that anyone who takes up his case sympathetically will get a lot of shit publicity from the hang 'em high mob, internet trolls et cetera, so I did myself a favour too.'

I bought him a second pint (his Green sympathies led him to drink only the artisan draught which was much more expensive that the other beers on offer). He asked me about my temporary post at the university which had come to an end. I told him I was relieved as the academic life had been a mistake.

'Get out while you can,' he advised. 'As a neuro linguistic programmer I can tell you that the longer you stay in academia the worse the effect on you. Me, I love it. It's my showbiz.'

After I got behind his camp exterior, I actually found the man's showy frankness quite entertaining. Perhaps McDade had missed a trick in not letting Dunnet write a sympathetic study of his disfunctional life, but I wouldn't have been sure that Jason might have been tempted by 'beautiful Billy' and got a hatchet in his head for his trouble.

CHAPTER 9

My third meeting that day was with Adrian Frei. He had asked me to come to his flat on the Waterfront. I took the tram which now extends to Newhaven and had time to buy a bottle of wine at the large Asda which sits across the dock from the Western Harbour flats in which he lives. The front room of his flat was lined with well-filled bookcases on opposite sides, and a large window looked west over the Firth of Forth. It had a good view of the Forth Bridges over which the sun was now setting. He gratefully accepted my proffered bottle of wine but offered me a malt whisky which I accepted.

When I saw a copy of the famous menu on top of his breakfast bar, I did not need to ask him if he had dropped his. Of course he might have picked up another one but the more he talked the less likely he seemed to be as a suspect. He was a stout, short man with a shiny bald patch and the watery eyes of a habitual drinker. He dropped some Oxford names into the conversation (as I had been told he might), offered me a copy of his latest crime thriller (self-published but available on Amazon) and was surprisingly generous about the four famous writers. I got the impression that the 'puff' piece he had written for his Sunday newspaper column was sincere and perhaps he had been misjudged. The apparent enmity between him and the Book Festival lady who had attended the dinner was perhaps not his fault as the literary world can be as bitchy as any other.

To my surprise he showed enthusiasm for the idea of a Tuesday Talk and even suggested a title: 'Villainy and the Supernatural in literature'. I thought it was an excellent theme and accepted right away. I was also relieved I did not have the embarrassment of finding an excuse to withdraw the false invitation which had secured me this meeting. My main purpose, however, was to find out about his visit to Longforgan.

'Ah,' he sighed. 'That was a big mistake. As you may know I try my hand at crime fiction, alas without much success, and I had an idea for a true crime book. It seemed a good idea when I learned McDade was on a release schedule and I thought I would not have any difficulty gaining access to him in that other prison. I was quite excited to meet him. It seemed to me that if the likes of Dr Forbes-Graham had cleared him for release, he would be willing to talk to me and be amenable to the idea. I even offered him a choice of ghost writing it for him, doing a joint book with both our names on it, or writing up his story in my words. But I got quite a shock when I did meet him. In fact I found him quite frightening. He stood looking at me with those cold blue eyes and said nothing. Eventually he reacted to the choices I had suggested and said 'No, no and no' in a quiet voice that was quite sinister. He added that if I went ahead without him I would have to answer to him for the consequences. That was what frightened me. Being actually threatened to my face by a known psychopathic killer is not something I had experienced before.' He laughed nervously.

'So you withdrew the offer?'

'Oh yes, I wrote to him the next day and said I had no intention of writing anything about him and he could be assured of that. Crikey, I know I can write some strong stuff sometimes in my criticisms (pen mightier than the sword and all that) but I'm really a coward at heart and I like to sleep at night.'

Having now met the man, I was pretty sure that Adrian Frei was not the villain we were looking for. I think the 'Oxon cube' was a lonely man and lacked friends in his adopted home of Edinburgh. He needed an audience for his books to make him feel popular and I could at least supply him with one. I suggested a couple of potential dates for his Tuesday Talk and got the tram back to Haymarket. Rosie was still up, waiting for my report.

I told her that I was now certain Frei was innocent, as was Dunnet. She shuddered when I recounted the little jibes I had endured through lunch with Forbes-Graham and roared with rage when I told her he described me as her 'latest squeeze'. Together we looked up Sir Martin on the internet to see if we could get further information about him.

His marriage to Louise Loudon, the Human Rights lawyer and life peer appeared to have been contracted only a few years previously. I wonder if she had discovered his true feelings about human being as 'animals' and if the distance between London and Edinburgh helped keep their marriage together for appearance's sake. He had held a professorship in forensic psychiatry in Wales before being appointed to Carstairs where he was still a visiting consultant, until he took early retirement to chair a public enquiry on deaths in police custody which had received widespread coverage in the media and at which Dame Louise Loudon had appeared as a witness. They conducted a short long distance courtship and married soon after. She retained her flat in Pimlico and he his house in the new development of the former Donaldson School for the Deaf, just west of Haymarket. The large square turreted old building was turned into flats and round the rear of the spacious grounds a crescent of new town houses had been constructed. He (and occasionally they) lived in one of these.

'I'll bet he paid for his town house out of that public enquiry,' Rosie muttered. 'He would have got a hefty sum from an enquiry that went on for months. Needlessly I may add. Most of the verdicts could be done with a pile of newspaper cuttings in a fraction of the time. At the Bar we don't protest too much because we can get weeks of work out of it, trawling through witnesses who have nothing new to say. All paid for out of the public purse to create an impression of concern about some tragedy.'

'You sound cynical.'

'Maybe I am but I was delighted to get an all inclusive holiday in Turkey out of the Trams Public Enquiry,' she grinned.

'Here's something interesting.' I was looking at the footnotes in the Wikipedia entry on Forbes-Graham. 'He qualified in hypnotherapy after his psychiatric qualification. That gives me an idea. Suppose he has a patient, let's call him Billy, who gets a kick out of killing. He spends hours giving him 'treatment', only he is like a Svengali, building up control over the boy to make him into an assassin. Normal humans would perhaps revolt at being trained up in this way, but not Billy. Svengali provides him with the targets, the method and the tools to finish the job. Sir Martin himself isn't anywhere near when the deed is done, and his fingerprints and DNA are carefully kept off the weapons. Maybe he even trains Billy to use gloves and cover his tracks. That could be the answer linking Balaclava man to the menu doodler.'

'Yes, but it doesn't tell us why he wanted these writers dead. There must be a motive surely.'

'Maybe he gets a kick of doing this to people he

despises. We know he hates crime writers and he sees all this as a chess game in which he acts as Grand Master. I told you that I felt I was being played over lunch. Patronised and played.'

'What if Billy gets caught? Won't he spill the beans?'

'Billy is ideal. He is a cold fish who looks like one of the Midwich cuckoos. He doesn't talk very much. Suppose Svengali has hypnotised him to forget the sessions, and say that the voices told him to do these murders. It could work that way. What's more if they come to Svengali and ask what was going on in those sessions he can't and he won't talk. 'Patient confidentiality',' I mimicked Sir Martin's accent.

'So Sir Martin, the Svengali, assembles all the kit for the murders and gives it to Billy and tells him what to do, to whom and where and when. That calls for them to meet together or have some form of communication which doesn't incriminate the mastermind. I haven't worked that bit out yet and we need Helen and her team to help us with information.' I could see Rosie shaking her head, but I was on a roll. 'Let me make a call.'

In my capacity as 'janitor', I had the numbers on my phone of all the therapists who worked out of rooms they rent in the Arthur Conan Doyle Centre, two of whom were hypnotherapists. I called Douglas Young, the first number. It was 11pm and I apologised for calling so late.

'Is everything OK at the Centre, Max? There's not been fire or anything?'

I knew he kept his patient records in a locked cabinet and would not appreciate losing them. I outlined my scenario and asked if such a procedure could work on a willing subject, especially one who was a psychopath. I said it was to settle an argument.

'Yes, it could. It is common in some treatments of trauma to suggest to the patient that they will forget what has happened during the session when they wake up. In other cases – if the subject is a good one or been trained over several sessions – to implant a post-hypnotic action which they must follow at a certain time in a certain way. I have seen that work many times. The subject does not know why they did something when asked afterwards, and has no recollection that it came via hypnosis.'

'That's great, Douglas. Many thanks. You can go to sleep now!'

He laughed and thankfully did not ask any more.

I turned to Rosie. 'Can I ask a favour, please. Call Helen, she'll answer when she sees your number. Ask her to meet me for breakfast at the Woodpecker Cafe at 8 o'clock. My treat. We need to get moving before Billy tries again.'

She agreed and the rendezvous was made. I did not dare guess what gruff response she got from the feisty detective.

CHAPTER 10

Helen Dyer was waiting for me (in uniform) when I arrived at the Woodpecker Café. I used to go there sometimes with a group of my students after our seminars. It's at a corner of St Leonard's Street not far from Dumbiedykes in the east end of the city centre. The former church building in which it occupies the ground floor, on an upper level houses the woodworking workshop in which McDade was now apparently working. The Woodpecker Project gives work and skills to those who need a new start in life by teaching them the techniques of working with materials, principally wood, as the name suggests. That part of the project can be reached by a stair inside the cafe, and also by a small door outside on St Leonard's Street. I intended to try to talk to the Project manager with Helen present.

We ordered breakfast and carried mugs of tea to a table in the corner while it was being cooked. Helen did not need to say 'Max, this had better be good' - her expression said it for her. She waited while I explained why I had asked her there. I gave her as full an account of my meetings with the three men the previous day as I could, and reasoned why I thought Sir Martin Forbes-Graham was now the most likely suspect.

'You know, Max, I could report you as interfering in a police investigation but since you gave us the original lead, I obviously won't. But I will be duty bound to pass on any information you have to the new SIO on the case, DCS Durrant.'

'Thank you. Please do that. Do you know anything about hypnotism?'

'No, why?'

I gave her the information about the psychiatrist being adept at it, and what the professional hypnotherapist had told me. 'That would explain how he managed to control McDade and get him to commit the murders. Sorry, attempted murders.'

'Always assuming Balaclava Man is McDade' said Helen. We have no evidence to suggest he is, so we can't bring him in or search his place. I wish we could get permission to trace his mobile phone locations but even if he is out on parole, we will have difficulty in getting the warrant. I have the number as he is required to be available to his parole officer, and I know where he is staying - in a crummy flat in Dumbiedykes. I gather he comes here in the evenings to work on his sculptures.'

'Good, that means he will not be upstairs in the workshop now. Do you mind coming with me to talk to the manager when we finish our breakfast?'

'Perhaps. What do you intend to ask him?'

'That I heard the famous sculptor is working here and I was interested in commissioning him something. I believe they sell the work done here for charity.'

'And why would I be there?'

'You're a friend of mine and together we are funding a bust of Rosie in wood, as a surprise for her. In fact you don't have to say anything. Your uniform will do the talking, or rather encourage him to talk.'

'You're a devious devil, Max. But I'll do it. I agree with you that McDade is a likely suspect but there's very little we can do until we have evidence. He could claim we are harassing him while he's on parole. Remember he has some powerful backers.'

We went upstairs to the upper floor, and then down another internal stair to the small office of the Project manager with a door onto St Leonard's Street. His name was Marvin Wilde and he couldn't have been more welcoming...until I mentioned the name of McDade.

'Must it be him? I mean we have other gifted wood workers. Billy has only recently come to us and he now only works in the evenings after the other volunteers leave.'

The hours he worked were of course irrelevant but I sensed there was something behind it and I pressed him. 'Was there a problem?'

'Well,' he hesitated. 'There was actually....I don't

want to get Billy into trouble or anything, especially with the police but there was an incident...' He glanced at Helen before continuing. 'When Billy came we were delighted. His work is already well recognised and would bring us credit and publicity. His sponsor wrote to us and said he was entitled to a second chance. Which is one of the things we believe here. He used to carry a Gideon Bible with him – you know the brown ones you find in hotel rooms - and it seemed very precious to him.'

'Would the sponsor be Sir Martin Forbes-Graham?' I interrupted.

'Yes. When Billy joined us we thought he might encourage some of the people who come on Friday to a starter class, but he was remarkably untalkative. He just stared and said very little. And then there was an unfortunate incident....look, I don't want this to go any further, please. One of the volunteer waitresses in the cafe, a very pretty student came up with coffees for the group on a tray. She came back later to collect the cups when only Billy was left in the workshop. He ...well, he pushed her against the wall and put her hand on his jeans and...well, he had an erection. She ran downstairs and spoke to the supervisor and he later told me about the episode. We felt that in order to avoid bad publicity for the project and not to jeopardise his parole, we would get him to work alone in the evenings. The girl agreed not to make a complaint and we promised her that she would not be on shift when he was around...and that's how it is. Not ideal but we don't want to ask him to leave. Well, not yet anyway.'

'Thanks for telling us, Marvin. I appreciate it and we won't say anything. But in view of the fact that the bust we had in mind is of a very attractive lady who would have to do sittings with the sculptor I think perhaps we will rethink.'

He was obviously disappointed to lose the commission but showed us around the workshop in case we changed our minds and opted for another sculptor. My bust idea had been fictitious but the more I thought about it the more appealing it became.

'It may seem a strange thing to ask, Marvin, but did Billy McDade have an injured arm?'

'Yes, he did. He had a bandage round his forearm. Apparently a neighbour's dog bit him. But it didn't stop him working.'

Another piece of evidence linking McDade with the attack on Caitlin Mossiman had fallen into place. Helen smiled her approval at me. When we got outside she was anxious to get away but I asked if she would mind telling me one more thing.

'Can you please send me the locations of the crime writers whose homes were targeted. I have the one for Queen Street Gardens already but publishers don't usually give out home addresses, understandably. I promise I will not contact them in any way.'

'Yes I suppose I could, but what's that got to do with anything?'

'I'd like to see where they live. Do you have the What3Words app on your phone, Helen? You could give them to me that way.'

'As a matter of fact I do have it. When I climb a mountain and break my ankle I can give the rescue team a 5 by 5 metre square in which to find me.'

I knew she was not joking as she was a dedicated rambler and hillwalker. She and Rosie had done a couple of 'Munroes' (the Scottish mountains over 3000 feet) together, and I had been invited on their next expedition.

'I'll send them if you promise me, Max, that you will not speak to them or go near McDade in the meantime.' I agreed and we parted.

I went back to the West End and got Rosie's car from the residents' permit spaces outside her flat. It was the day to collect Tom from Longforgan and I had plenty of time to do it.

The bureaucratic process for the release from prison, especially an 'open' one, was easier than I thought it would be, and we were soon on the road back to Edinburgh. I took him to the hostel in which Rosie had billeted him. It was a former church at the foot of Palmerston Place and would do until he found his feet and possible employment. He seemed nervous of going to her flat before she arrived back from her court case so I took him first to the ACD Centre and my own flat. He had hardly any personal possessions so I gave him some shirts and corduroy trousers until he could acquire a wardrobe of his own, plus a pack of slips as underwear. He and I were about the same built but he would use less notches on the belt. Then we went round to Rosie's flat and waited for her to arrive with our meal. I was sure that after eating I should leave the two of them to have time together, but the delay gave us a chance to speak more personally.

'I appreciate this, Max. You could have easily seen me as a nuisance getting in the way of your friendship with Rosie.'

'I don't. But I won't deny I would be upset if she gets hurt in any way. Your appearance was a shock. She did her best when you were born and she doesn't deserve to feel any guilt.'

'I know, and she's now the only person I have. I'm the one who should feel guilty, especially about my adoptive parents in Greenock. I put them through a lot and now they have more sorrows. I don't blame them for severing the connection. Perhaps I can make it up in some way.'

I didn't know how to respond. I didn't like the idea that Rosie was all he had. It sounded self-pitying. His conviction was for smooth-talking people out of money. After all he was twenty years old and surely he had other friends before he went to prison. I suggested he should not rush into trying to see his adoptive parents again. Perhaps a letter of remorse and sympathy for their situation. That would do no harm.

The door opened and Rosie was home. She had collected a Chinese meal from the Rendezvous in Queensferry Street on her way and we opened a bottle of white to go with it. The evening was going well. Mother and son seemed more relaxed as it went on, and I felt as if I should now leave them alone.

'No, Max, I need to get to the hostel and settle in. I'll see you tomorrow, as we agreed in the car.'

When he left, Rosie grew tense again. 'What is it you and Tom are doing tomorrow?'

I told her that I had asked him if he would come with me to the Woodpecker project and try to open a conversation with McDade in the workshop while I waited downstairs in the cafe in case it did not go well. I explained my plan,'Tom has met him before and can pretend to want advice on where to find work. He can ask him about Forbes-Graham and it might lead to information that the police will never get out of him. They can't even take him for questioning. They have nothing on him at the moment. Only what we have put together.'

'What YOU have put together, Max. I don't like it. Billy is a psycho whatever gloss that lying Forbes-Graham may have put on it for his own ends. What if he feels cornered? Tom may have a glib tongue but that counts for nothing with psychos. Believe me I have had them for clients. Scum who deserve to be taken off this earth, but we're not allowed to say that now.'

I had not heard her talk like that before and could tell she was on edge. I tried to reassure her that Tom and I would have our mobiles open on WhatsApp and at the slightest sign of trouble he would exit or I would intervene.

'McDade does not know what I look like so I can be there without him making a connection between us.'

'I still don't like, Max. Will you forgive me if I want to be alone tonight. I appreciate all you did today. Collecting Tom and giving him something for his wardrobe. But I need to think about what I need to do about Tom and how much I can allow him into my life. Sorry.' She kissed me long and tenderly, and I left her alone.

CHAPTER II

Helen had made good overnight on her promise to send me the addresses of the three crime writers. Caitlin Mossiman I already had. She had included as a bonus the street in which McDade had his one bedroom flat, in a set of run-down council houses to the south of Holyrood known as Dumbiedykes.

Over my muesli&fruit mix I wrote them all the locations down as three word codes. I like What3Words. It is a simple way of logging any 5x5 square metre spot in the world. It also offers an overhead satellite image as well the map location.

On the wall of my flat I had pinned a large scale map of Edinburgh which had helped me to reacquaint myself with the city of my schooldays and plot the bus routes. I put a red pin into each writer's home; a blue pin for the home of each of the three suspect dinner guests; and a yellow one in Dumbiedykes Road for McDade although I did not have the exact address. Finally I put one in the Woodpecker Café and workshop and noticed how near it was to McDade. Now if this was some esoteric murder mystery, they would form a swastika or some other sinister symbol and I would know the Nazis were behind it all. However, I was certain I knew who was behind it all, and none of our four writers would ever have come up with a plot so far-fetched.

What this exercise did do was give me an idea of how widespread the locations were around Edinburgh. From Flo Scott Thomas to Ronald MacKenzie in Leith Links, from Anton Ross in Colinton to Caitlin Mossiman in the New Town. I took out the pins for Dunnet and Frei, and noticed that Forbes-Graham lived a kilometre west of where I was in Palmerston Place and Rosie round the corner. I stared at the map, trying to imagine how Sir Martin managed it. How and where did he meet McDade to give him his instructions. I was certain that he was too clever to be seen with his vile protegé in a public place or to have him visit his home. Where did he store the materials and chemicals used for the attempted murders? Certainly not in McDade's flat. That would be too obvious for a self-styled mastermind. Perhaps a rented lock-up convenient for Billy boy. I knew the police were doing forensic and fingerprint checks on the murder materials that so far had yielded nothing or where they were bought and by whom. The sorcerer had trained his apprentice well. But they had to have some form of communication and it was my guess that it involved something like WhatsApp messages with end-to-end encryption, probably not unlike the way drug gangs use burner phones not registered to either party. Even if the police had checked the location of the registered mobile of McDade at the time of the attacks they would be unlikely to find anything, unless he had been foolish enough to take it with him. I was getting nowhere fast but it passed the time. I had a siesta snooze to freshen my mind and went to collect Tom Sanderson from the hostel. We walked up to Haymarket and took a bus which would drop us near to the Woodpecker. Sitting upstairs at the unoccupied rear of the bus, I explained my plan.

Tom had been gifted a mobile with pre-paid Tesco SIM by Rosie on which WhatsApp had been installed. We agreed we would both keep a channel open on WhatsApp and he would go upstairs from the Café where I would be seated. The plan was that he would find McDade in the Workshop, explaining that he had been told Billy was working there. Now that he was out of HMP Castle Huntly, Tom would explain, he was looking for someone in Edinburgh who could help him find work or give him some tips. It was an unlikely tale but it might just get McDade to say something that we could use. Naturally Tom would not introduce the name of Forbes-Graham right away.

I settled in with a white coffee as Tom set off upstairs. I had a Bluetooth earpiece linked to my phone which enabled me to hear the ensuing conversation more clearly. Tom knocked on the workshop door and greeted McDade who was obviously working on a wood sculpture and explained how he had found him and why he had come. Silence ensued. I could see in my mind's eye the Midwich cuckoo staring back at Tom, unwilling to engage. Tom tried again.

'Come on, Billy. Don't be like that. I only need a bit of help and advice. Look, I don't want money. My mother gave me plenty. If I give you a fiver would you go and get us a coffee from downstairs and let me look at your work? These wood carvings are bloody impressive.'

The compliment seemed to work and a few moments later McDade came down the stair into the cafe and walked past me to the counter. Never having met me, there was no chance he would recognise me. In my earpiece I heard Tom rustling through something. I had told him to pay particular attention to the Gideon Bible which Marvin Wilde had mentioned. McDade was served all too quickly and carried two mugs of coffee upstairs. A moment later I heard his voice, high-pitched and loud.

'Heh! Whit the hell are you daeing. Get yer fuckin' hands aff ma Bible!'

Disaster had struck and Tom was alone with an angry killer. I got up from my table and began to ascend the stairs. There was a scream in my earpiece. Tom's voice.

I burst into the workshop to find Billy McDade standing over Tom who lay on the floor on his back. There was a chisel in McDade's hand with blood on its blade.

When I entered the room he was still shouting at Tom. I shall never forget the sight and sound of these moments. His actual voice which I heard in front of me in the room was also coming like a weird echo through the earpiece linked to my phone.

'Think you could spy on me ye wee bastard. I'ts the last spying you'll dae.' He raised the chisel to strike again.

Before I could think twice, I had crossed the room, picking up one of the woodworking tools on the bench as I went.

I swung it at McDade and it struck him in his neck at the right side. Blood spurted everywhere as he collapsed in front of me. The tool I had swung at him had a blade like a sickle and it had been razor sharp. It had severed his carotid artery and I had killed him with one frenzied blow.

I sank to my knees in front of Tom. He was conscious but in obvious pain clutching his chest.

I found myself saying, 'It's OK, Tom. I've killed him, I'm getting you an ambulance.' (OK? Killed him? I had said those words, me who had never killed anything in my life.) I remember telling Tom to keep pressing on the wound to staunch the bleeding, dialling 999, running downstairs to the café and alerting them to look out for the ambulance. I remember seeing them take Tom away. Maybe I collapsed, fainted or blacked out, but the next thing I recall was being in a police station with a burly Glaswegian questioning me. Perhaps the paramedics who attended the scene had given me something for shock.

I was still not coherent but I was not going to lie. I told them what had happened. I had struck the blow which killed McDade. His blood was still all over my clothes and I could hardly deny it. The fact I had done it to prevent him killing Tom, or to prevent him turning on me seemed irrelevant as I was saying it. But of course that was what helped me later to avoid a murder or a manslaughter charge.

The burly Glaswegian turned out to be DCS David Durrant, Helen's boss and the new SIO of the crime writer attacks.

'We know you are telling the truth Max, because Tom Sanderson had his mobile set to record as well as to send you the conversation. We've heard it all and we're satisfied you acted to save his life - and possibly your own. McDade was a vicious killer when he went into Carstairs and he still was until you stopped him. I think you acted in good faith and I doubt if you will be charged.'

'But Tom Sanderson, what happened? Is he all right?'

The DCS' face darkened. 'I'm sorry I don't know. He went into A&E at the Western and he's still in surgery. There was internal bleeding and that's not good. Do you want to get checked over yourself?'

'No,' I said. 'He didn't lay a finger on me.' Then I burst into tears.

I was still sobbing when Helen Dyer came into the interview room and put an arm round me. 'Come on Max. You'd better get home and cleaned up. I'm afraid you'll have to leave these clothes and your phone here. I'll take you in a police car'.

I was still blubbering on the way and asked her how Rosie was, and did she know about Tom?

'Yes, she's at the hospital now but it's maybe best you don't go there or to her flat just yet. I'll drop by in the morning to see you're all right.'

As she left, the words 'just yet' came back to me to complete my emotional wreck, and a terrible feeling in the pit of my stomach reminded me that I had persuaded Tom to see McDade against her warnings. If he died she would be right to blame me for his death.

Chapter 12

Rosie spent most of the night at the Western General hospital where Tom fought for his life. She was persuaded to go home and get some sleep. When she opened her mailbox there was a letter from the Lord Advocate's office offering the sheriffdom she had coveted for so long. It was in Tayside. Such bitter sweet news to add to the trauma she was going through. She had been excused by the judge from appearing in the trial in which she had previously been involved, and her junior counsel, Marco Nardini took over.

It was not until 11 a.m. the next morning that the call came from the hospital. Tom was dying despite blood transfusions aplenty and she got there just in time, before he slipped away into death, leaving her in a mess of tears and heaving sobs. Helen had been given the day off by DCS Durrant to support her friend. The two of them returned to Rosie's flat and after persuading her to take a sleeping pill, Helen said she would go round the corner to break the news to me.

'I don't want to see Max,' Rosie apparently told her friend, and Helen passed this painful message when she arrived at my door. It was lunchtime but

I had not yet shaved. I was dishevelled and still, I admit it, in a state of shock.

'He died peacefully, Tom, and if it helps, he thanked Rosie and told her he loved her.'

Helps? I thought instead it would make Rosie's grief all the deeper and more difficult. She had been suspicious of Tom's motives in seeking her out. To have died with that declaration on his lips must be tearing at her heart. She had given him up as a baby and felt the pain of loss then. Now she had lost him again in terrible circumstances which I had been instrumental in creating. Our relationship would surely not survive this. But I wanted to try. I knew that I loved her and I wanted to support her in her loss, despite my role in taking Tom to that fatal encounter.

'Will she see me eventually, Helen? I feel terrible about Tom. I love her but I understand her anger.'

'I don't know, Max. She's sleeping now so I don't think you should go round. She loves you but I don't know how deeply. At the moment she blames you for taking Tom there, so I don't know how it will play. Maybe this evening but don't keep up your hopes. It's been a huge blow. The irony is that this tragedy came the same day as the letter offering her a sheriffdom in Tayside. What she always hoped for.'

I too had hoped it would happen and had even dreamt that I might move with her and find a new career, and perhaps become her life partner. That now looked to be shattered. I told Helen I was glad that this would enable Rosie to have a new start. I meant it, and the tears in my eyes were not only for myself.

I rose to show her out but she asked me to sit.

'I have something else to tell you, Max. Do you remember the last words that McDade said to Tom?'

'Something about 'get your hands off my Bible.' I asked Tom to see if he could have a look at the Gideon Bible McDade apparently was so attached to. It just didn't fit with his evil personality.'

'Well, when McDade went down for the coffees, Tom must have opened the Bible. It had been hollowed out inside by a chisel to create a compartment in which he kept a burner phone. The one he used to get his instructions from his Svengali. We looked through the phone and found only two apps: WhatsApp and What3Words. The WhatsApp had a series of voice messages from an undisclosed number which sounded like hypnotherapy sessions. We presume they put him into trance. They gave instructions how and when to commit the murders, all four of them, then told him he would find the locations of the tools 'at the usual place' and where the victims lived on the What3words app.'

'And was the voice on the messages that of Sir Martin Forbes-Graham, his mentor?'

'No, that's the devilish clever bit. It was one of these electronically created voices, not as naff as Stephen Hawking's, but ideal for putting him at ease. The other clever bit is that without the other phone we can't tell who was sending them. It was a burner that was switched off after each message. It meant the two men did not need to meet physically after he left prison. Svengali pulled his strings by phone, leaving no evidence the two were ever in the same place or room. Cunning, eh?'

'Yes. Planned minutely by a criminal mastermind who happens to be a forensic psychiatrist. He would have trained his pet killer to avoid fingerprints and DNA traces but even if McDade was caught at the scene of the crimes, it could not be traced to him. 'It wasn't me, it was 'The Voice' that told me to do it'. Very Peter Sutcliffe. Very clever and creepy.'

'The What3words messages came in on WhatsApp from the same phone.'

'And specified these four crime scenes?'

'Not only. One location cropped up several times – it was 'the usual place'. It turned out to be a rented lock-up not far from Dumbiedykes, near the Commonwealth Pool. Naturally we went straight there as we didn't need a warrant. We found the Balaclava; another knife (remember he dropped one in Queen Street Gardens), a camping gas cylinder, bottles of nitric acid, glycerine, potassium cyanide solution, a whole duplicate kit for the stuff he used to carry out the murder attempts. There were his fingerprints and DNA aplenty. And there's more. There was a bottle of wine – expensive vintage – perhaps if Anton Ross didn't drink his whisky it was for a second attempt, or maybe intended for another victim. We also found a bottle of acetone, a packet of condoms and a box of night light candles.'

'Presumably the condoms were for rapes McDade was hoping to commit.'

'Well no, actually. I'm glad you're sitting down Max, for this next bit. The acetone, condom and candle together make up a kit that arsonists sometimes use. They fill the condom with highly combustible accelerant, suspend it above the lit candle and when the rubber melts, it creates a mini inferno which spreads.'

'But there were no fire doodles on the menu.'

'No, but there was a recent voice message to the phone after you and I went to the Woodpecker Café and you had lunch with Doctor Death in the New Club. You must have really got under his skin, Max, when you asked him about McDade. Prepare yourself for a wee surprise. You see, the final What3Words location is right where we are sitting, or rather underneath it.' My jaw dropped.

'You mean I was a target?'

'Yep. Looks like it. You got too close and had made

the link. Not that we can prove that or connect him with the messages to McDade unless we get him in possession of the phone at the other end. He can easily deny everything. The message on the phone told Billy to creep in here during the day and hide until you locked up and went to bed, then set the fire and let himself out. But at least you don't have to worry about psycho McDade any more. You did a good job there, Max. I shall have to watch my tongue with you in future.' She grinned and left me to absorb all that she had told me.

CHAPTER 13

I left it until evening to try to speak to Rosie. I needed to do it in person. I shaved, showered to clear my head, and was about to buzz her entryphone when she emerged. I had never seen her looking like she was. Grief had made rings around her eyes which were dull and emotionless.

She recognised me and whirled round venomously.

'You bastard, don't come near me. You fucking got my son killed and you come creeping round here. Go away. I don't want to see you again.'

I staggered back, too shocked to reply. I have never heard her swear before and before I could reply, she turned sharp right and walked away. Beyond the west end of Eglinton crescent I saw the railings of the former Donaldson's School and suddenly guessed where she was heading, and possibly why.

I decided to follow at a discreet distance. It was already dark and I kept myself in shadow. She entered the development from the big gates on Wester Coates and walked up the road which curved around the vast lawn to the massive square shape of the former school and carried on beyond to the town houses behind. They were in the shape of a crescent and bounded on the north side by railings separating them from woods which dropped sharply down to the Water of Leith twenty metres below. It was as secluded a location as you could wish for, yet close to the Haymarket transport hub.

I saw Rosie approach the town house of Forbes-Graham. She stood outside, saying something into the camera of the entryphone. There was a pause, then a buzz. She pushed open the door and went inside.

I rushed forward to catch the door before it closed and held it open a fraction until Rosie had disappeared upstairs. There was no doubt in my mind that she was in danger and in no state of mind to defend herself. I knew I had to intervene. I closed the door quietly and stole up the lush stair carpet towards the voices coming from upstairs. I crept up to a point outside the lounge from which I could see them both through the slit between the partly open door and its frame.

Sir Martin's voice dominated with its upper-class assured tones.

'This is a surprise, Rosamunde. I won't pretend it is a happy occasion. Both of us have suffered losses yesterday. Allow me to express condolences on the loss of your son. My loss is maybe not as great as yours but I was fond of young Billy and delighted he had made such great progress since Carstairs. I understand that he was killed by your friend

Max Quillan.' Always the provocation, to put his interlocutor on the defensive.

Rosie brushed his remark aside and spoke in a voice hoarse with emotion. 'It was YOU who killed my son by proxy. Your evil little pet killer may have stabbed him but I know you were behind it, and the murder attempts on these famous authors. I know what a clever bastard you have been. The police will find it difficult to prove how you controlled Billy McDade. You know as well as I do, the legal rules that anything you tell me will not be admissible as evidence against you. I have no recording device on me. I am not 'wired' as the police might say. You can search me. I just want to know one thing. Why did you want to kill those people?'

'Please, Rosamunde. Sit down so that we can discuss this properly. I think we both need a drink. What can I offer you, a whisky? Brandy?'

He turned his back on Rosie and poured two brandies into bell-shaped glasses from a decanter on a marble topped drinks cabinet. Through the slit in the door I could see him add something from a small bottle into one of the glasses. He handed it to Rosie.

To my dismay Rosie drank from her glass. She probably needed the effect of the alcohol and in her distressed state would not have suspected he had spiked her glass. No doubt he had used the trick before, and what violated woman would be able to make the charge stick that the distinguished Sir Martin had drugged and raped her?

Alas I saw that I was right in my suspicion when he suddenly became very frank and admitted everything, and the more he admitted the less chance Rosie had of leaving alive.

'You defend criminals, Rosie, I treat them as patients. But the people I despise most are the authors who make millions, trotting out silly stories making the police into heroes. They are dolts. So I decided to play a game using Billy, I admit. Yes, it was a Great Game. He found it exciting and so did I. There was, as you have observed, no way of tracing my connection to him. I supplied all the equipment and chemicals, rented a lock-up under a false name and left him anonymous instructions. As he was my former patient I would not have been able to discuss his case if questioned. If he were to be caught, then everyone (or most people until you and your pal Max came along) would assume he had gone back to his murderous tendencies.'

At this point I could see that Rosie's head had dropped forward. She tried to speak but a slurred expression came out.

'Oh dear, I see I put too much Rohypnol in your brandy. I'd better be quick to tell you that I will make sure you don't suffer. I'll take your keys and help you back to your flat where your grief at losing Tom will overcome you so much, that you will hang yourself from your lovely high ceiling rose. Four metres high I think, but I will manage to use the chandelier which is lower than that.' He advanced towards her and for the second time in two days I found myself attacking a murderer.

I burst into the room and he looked up, shocked. 'You!' he managed to say before I launched myself at his throat. The strength in my hands was not my own and he was a good ten years older than me. I squeezed until he struggled no more. I didn't know if he was still unconscious or already dead. I found a length of washing line in the kitchen cupboard and wound it around his neck, covering any bruises I had made in strangling him. I was about to do to him what he would have done to her and I was damned if I would stand trial for killing him.

Rosie was deeply asleep on the settee by now. The adrenaline kept me going as I set about the task of faking Sir Martin's suicide. I looked for his mobile phone and saw it lying on the table. I scrolled through the contacts and found the number for Louise, his wife. I typed a cryptic message: 'Billy McDade all my fault. I can't live with it any longer' and sent it. I wiped the phone, pressed it into the limp hand of Sir Martin to get his prints, then put it back on the lounge table.

The central rose in the ceiling was a lot lower than

the one in Rosie's flat but I decided not to emulate what he was intending to do to her. Crossing my fingers that any security system (if there was one) would not be recording because the householder was at home, I dragged his body to the stairwell, put a chair beside the railing on the top landing and tied the line around it before heaving Sir Martin over.

I popped Rosie's brandy glass into a plastic bag to take away with me, having flushed its contents down the loo. Lifting her up by her armpits I managed to get her downstairs and we staggered like a couple of drunks across the Donaldson's development and out onto the main thoroughfare of Wester Coates where I hailed a passing taxi on its way to the rank at Haymarket.

'Sorry my wife had too much to drink,' I lied to the driver.

It's said people in a coma can sometimes hear what is said to them and I hoped that Rosie could not hear me. The taxi dropped us at her door and I tipped the man heavily. Using her keys to get into her flat, I put her to bed and went back to my own flat in the ACD building. It was only when I got inside that I started shaking. No tears this time. No regrets either. I knew that I could tell no one what I had done, not even Rosie who had been unconscious throughout.

Sir Martin's death was reported in the morning as 'breaking news'. After receiving the text message from her husband Lady Loudon had got in touch with the Edinburgh police who had discovered his body. The bit that relieved me most were the magic words 'police are not treating the death as suspicious'. One smart reporter had made the link with the death of McDade the previous day: 'Police would not confirm whether Sir Martin had taken his own life but it was well known that he had mentored the convicted rapist and murderer William 'Billy' McDade, recently freed from prison who since his release was suspected of four attacks on prominent writers and the death of a man in the Woodpecker Café in Edinburgh two days ago.'

The buzzer outside the door to my flat sounded. For the second day running I found DCI Helen Dyer on the doorstep of my little flat.

'Have you heard the news?' she asked.

'Yes, it was on the radio. How is Rosie taking it?'

'I don't know. I have just come from there and she looks like a zombie. She told me she thought of going round to his place last night and telling him that she would not rest until his role in all this was exposed and he was brought to justice.'

'And did she? Go, I mean?' I asked disingenuously.

'That's what's strange. She remembers leaving her flat, shouting at you on the front doorstep and walking away from you. The next thing she remembers is waking up this morning with the mother and father of a hangover and headache. She can't remember how she got home or when. Says she dreamed that Sir Martin confessed to her but she can't recall the details...Max, do you know anything about this?'

I'm not a good liar, especially to the police, but on this occasion I think I got away with it. I shook my head and kept my lie brief. 'No. How's Rosie now?'

'Not much better. She's had a helluva two days and it's no surprise she's not thinking straight. Look, I know it's not my business but she told me she said some terrible things to you outside her flat. I think she regrets that, but you'll need to give her time.'

'Can I come to Tom's funeral, or is it private?'

'I'll let you know. Take care.'

With that she left, but I never heard from her again.

CHAPTER 14

I had been lucky, I suppose. It looked as if Sir Martin's 'suicide' was being accepted as such by everyone. DCI Helen Dyer, however, was well aware of the role that he had played in the attempted murders and it was her duty to tell the Senior Investigating Officer what she had learned about Sir Martin Forbes-Graham. This would lead to the case being continued even though both prime suspects were dead.

As I had learned when he questioned me, DCS David Durrant was a gruff but decent man. He was also a proud Glaswegian and his temporary 'exile' (as he referred to it) to Glasgow's rival city of 'fur coats and nae knickers' to be SIO in the crime writers case, had not been to his liking. He took command because he was asked to. The daily commute and the difficulty of running an investigation with someone else's team were, he hoped, now at an end with the prime suspect dead. He could return to his home and family in Glasgow. Yet he knew that McDade must have had help or direction to have assembled the equipment in the lock-up garage. Nor could the detailed knowledge of the victims' habits and homes have been acquired by someone fresh out of prison.

When the burner phone hidden in McDade's bible was examined by his team it demonstrated clearly the role of a controlling person, as yet unknown.

When Helen Dyer told her boss about McDade's link to Forbes-Graham, first at Carstairs then at Castle Huntly, the forensic psychiatrist seemed to be an ideal candidate. He was qualified in hypnotherapy and the messages found in the phone were clearly hypnotic induction. He had been at the table where the marked menu had been dropped. She also relayed to Durrant that during lunch with me Forbes-Graham had told me he despised crime writers. But it was all circumstantial. That included his suicide which at face value might really have been remorse over mentoring McDade, or an attempt to escape exposure. The DCS was also well aware of the political and media minefield the case posed. Celebrity writers, a top forensic doctor with a wife in the House of Lords, and the fall-out that the release from prison of a crazed killer was posing for the prison service and politicians. Glasgow seemed further away than the forty five miles it actually was.

' Helen, what physical evidence do we have linking Forbes-Graham to McDade?' Durrant asked.

'None, sir. We haven't been able to trace where the items in the lock-up were bought or by whom. They must have been put there waiting for McDade to use. The key was possibly posted to him. There is no evidence that the two ever met after he left HMP Castle Huntly. But there is one item that could make the link – the burner phone used to send the voice messages and the What3words locations. If we can find that in the townhouse we could prove Svengali was Forbes-Graham.'

'Ah yes, the townhouse. Lady Loudon KC is there just now. She came up from London when we found the body. Are you familiar with the lady?'

'Only from seeing her on television bellyaching about the rights of criminals.'

'Couldn't have put it better myself, Helen. And what do you think her reaction will be if we buzz over there and ask if we can turn the place upside down to look for this phone?'

'Yessir. I can guess.'

'Why, she will ask. To look for evidence that your husband was an evil killer, we will say. Oh no, she will say, he's not yet in his grave and you are trashing his distinguished reputation. How do you think that will enhance our not-so-distinguished reputations with our friends in the judiciary? Digging up the real reason for his suicide will suit no one in the legal establishment or government. Eh, Helen?'

'I agree, but isn't it our duty to follow this up?'

'Yes it is, but it is not our responsibility to make the decision. I think this is one of the few times in my career that I will creep upstairs to the hierarchy and be guided by their wisdom.' He smiled sardonically as he said the word 'wisdom.' 'You see, there are a lot of people who will be hurt if all the facts about this case are made public . Let's take your friend Rosamunde Michelle KC soon to be a sheriff. If it was known that she gave up for adoption the son she had in her teens, and that the son later became a convicted felon who was killed in the Woodpecker Café by her boyfriend Max Quillan, it might delay her appointment. Certainly wouldn't help her image.'

Helen was shocked to discover how much DCS Durrant knew about Rosie, herself and Max. She had not told him, but he did not get to his rank without being a good detective.

The Chief Superintendent went on, 'And there's this fellow Max Quillan. He's been jolly helpful to us, interpreting the marks on the menu, tipping you off and tracing the connection between McDade and Forbes-Graham and, may I add, chopping off the monster's head. But what if his role is investigated in detail and I receive an order from on high to charge him with the unlawful killing of McDade? Then Helen, there's you, linked to both these people. That won't look good if all the details come out. ACC Barton brought me in to replace you as SIO not because you were at fault but because you were vulnerable by personal involvement with the aforementioned two. Finally, let me accuse myself.

How do I look as an SIO if I have to rely on a bloody medieval historian to find and follow up all the clues? Then he kills the prime suspect. Not charging Quillan and closing the case is a way to let us all off the hook.'

He looked at Helen with a strange smile. 'Do you still want to turn Forbes-Graham's house over to look for that phone?'

Helen Dyer returned the look. 'No, maybe it would be wise to rely on the wisdom of the others you spoke about.'

'It means accepting that McDade was cleverer than we know he really was, assembling all that kit in his lock-up. Apparently he was so clever he sent himself all those messages, using an AI bot to create the voice so that he would have an alibi. If no one believed he was hearing voices in his head telling him to kill crime writers – the Sutcliffe defence – then there was the proof on his phone. It wisnae' me, it wis the manny on the phone,' he mimicked. 'All shite of course but with both the bad guys dead, it will enable us to wind up the case without harming the people I have mentioned. You can have your team back and I can get back to Glasgow.'

He stood up to go.

DCS Durrant's solution suited everyone involved. Whether it was to hush up a scandal or not, no one challenged the story that Sir Martin had committed suicide, nor probed too deeply into his link to McDade. A journalist made a television documentary about the case and Durrant gave him the sanitised version in an interview. When it was aired, the conclusions only served to substantiate the motive for Sir Martin's suicide, namely remorse that he had failed to see that McDade might kill again if released.

Forbes-Graham's wife, the Human Rights champion, would also have suffered reputational damage if the truth had come out. If there ever had been a public enquiry into such an affair, the irony was that the person chosen to lead it would have been someone like Lady Loudon or Sir Martin.

The crime writers were never told of the role that a 'Svengali' might have played and seemed content that with the death of McDade they were no longer under threat. Helen got nice letters from all of them.

I don't know what happened about Tom's funeral and I did not contact either Rosie or Helen to ask. The days passed. I saw Rosie once in the street but she walked on by as though we were strangers. She had a new life to begin and I had to find a new career. Avenging angel is not a known occupation.

THE END